The Christmas Shoes

**Center Point
Large Print**

**This Large Print Book carries the
Seal of Approval of N.A.V.H.**

The Christmas Shoes

Donna VanLiere

CENTER POINT PUBLISHING
THORNDIKE, MAINE

This Center Point Large Print edition
is published in the year 2005 by arrangement with
St. Martin's Press.

Grateful acknowledgment is made for permission to reprint the
following: "The Christmas Shoes" by Eddie Carswell and
Leonard Ahlstrom copyright © 2000 Sony/ATV Songs LLC and
WB Music Corp./Jerry's Haven Music. All rights on behalf of
Sony/ATV Songs LLC administered by Sony/ATV Music
Publishing, 8 Music Square West, Nashville, TN 37203. All rights
on behalf of WB Music Corp./Jerry's Haven Music administered
by WB Music Corp. All rights reserved. Used by permission.

The text of this Large Print edition is unabridged. In other
aspects, this book may vary from the original edition. Printed in
Thailand. Set in 16-point Times New Roman type.

ISBN 1-58547-642-0

Library of Congress Cataloging-in-Publication Data

VanLiere, Donna, 1966-
    The Christmas shoes / Donna VanLiere.--Center Point large print ed.
    p. cm.
    ISBN 1-58547-642-0 (lib. bdg. : alk. paper)
    1. Large type books. I. Title.

PS3622.A66C48 2005
813'.6--dc22

                                                                2005006560

9172

For Troy,
who always encourages, always inspires,
always believes

The Christmas Shoes

ACKNOWLEDGMENTS

Troy, thank you for continuing to challenge and inspire me to new heights. I love you for giving me the courage to follow my dreams.

Eddie Carswell, Billy Goodwin, and the members of NewSong for inspiring this book. Your beautiful song has—and will—continue to touch millions of hearts around the world.

Helga Schmidt provided the beautiful true inspiration behind NewSong's lyrics. Helga, thank you for your tender heart and for sharing your moving story. You have left all of us forever changed.

From its earliest form, Jennifer Gates has shown nothing but unwavering belief in this book and given me constant guidance and encouragement. It wouldn't have happened without you. . . . I hope we can do it again!

Jennifer Enderlin and the staff at St. Martin's Press, thank you for your enthusiasm and for going the extra mile to get this book out quickly!

Esmond Harmsworth (and the Zachary Shuster Harmsworth Agency), Mark Maxwell and Don Zachary, thank you for your countless hours and incredible insight.

Deborah Chiel read the story again and again and provided invaluable input. Thank you.

It's a blessing to know that there are still people like

Eddie and Terri Carswell in the world. We hope to grow up to be just like you . . . really.

To other supporters, family, and friends: my parents, my mother- and father-in-law, Dave and Vicki, who have always loved me like one of their own, the ladies of Monday night, Vince Wilcox, Brian Smith and the Turning Point staff, Bob and Dannah Gresh, Paul Grimshaw, and George King, Dean Diehl, Jimmy Wheeler, Jackie Marushka, Benjie Gentry, and all of the Reunion Records, Provident, and Jive Records staffs. Thank you for your tremendous help.

And finally, thank you to Bailey, my faithful writing companion, for keeping me company and providing nothing but positive feedback.

PREFACE

Today

Some people go their entire lives missing the small miracles that happen throughout the day—those small blessings God sends from heaven to make us smile, laugh, or to break our hearts, and gently nudge us closer to His side.

I used to miss those tiny miracles: my children's giggles, their first awkward steps—their little hands wrapped gingerly around my fingers for support. I missed the sense of renewal as one season changed into the next: our dogwoods' scrawny limbs exploding into magnificent blossoms each spring, and summers when the giant oaks in our backyard dressed themselves in thick foliage, shading our home. I never noticed my wife's warm glances and easy laugh. I missed the blessing of her love for me.

One night, when joy was far away, God's grace touched me and opened my eyes. That same grace has inspired me to write this story, to share with you some of the things I have learned, though it's true, no one could have told me any of this then.

We all have questions in this life. It's taken me a long time to figure out what the really important questions are, the ones that matter. Not *How am I going to make enough money?* or *What can I do to get promoted?* No, more like *What are the flowers thinking beneath the snow? When do birds make reservations to fly south? What is God's plan for my life? What are my wife's dreams?*

A year ago I was finally able to connect all of the pieces. I met a young man who told me how it all happened. Now I know the truth, because now I know how God's hand guided my life.

Some people, perhaps someone like you, may write off this story as coincidence—a chance encounter, the random crossing of two lives. There was a time, just a few years ago, when I would have said the same. Back then you could not have convinced me that God would use a pair of shoes to change someone's life. But now I believe.

I most definitely believe.

God gave us the greatest proof of love that
the world has ever seen.
—Andrew Murray

PROLOGUE

Christmas Day, 2000

That winter, Christmas arrived without snow, which for our town was quite unusual. The fall had been beautiful, sunny and mild. People were in shirtsleeves at Thanksgiving. However, as the holiday season approached, nature turned, bringing, instead of blizzards, some of the worst ice storms of the century, coating everything with ice and knocking down trees and power lines. Then the weather turned bitterly cold, and stayed dark and grim, as everyone waited for the White Christmas Bing Crosby was dreaming of on all the local jukeboxes.

The sedan's tires spun on the ice, groping for solid ground. I put the car in reverse, backed up, turned the wheels at a different angle, put the car in drive, and attempted the hill into the cemetery a second time. This time the car climbed halfway up, but then the tires began to hum loudly, spinning again. I gave the car more gas but to no avail. Shifting into neutral, I released the clutch and let the car ease backward to the base of the hill, where I parked and turned off the engine.

From where I sat, I could see that the tombstone was covered with a brilliant sheen of ice. Icicles hung off

17

the sides, and brown leaves sat in frozen clusters on the cold stone. I would have to clean it off before I could decorate. I decided to leave everything in the trunk until I cleared the site.

As I got out of the car, the wind shrieked, cutting at my face. I pulled my wool overcoat tightly around me and picked up my gloves from the front seat. Realizing I'd left my hat at home, I pulled up my coat collar as high around my neck as I could and closed the car door behind me. I shivered and began the short climb up the hill.

Walking the hill was not much easier than driving it. I had to place my steps carefully to avoid slipping on the ice. As I entered the park, I could see that most of the pathways that wove throughout the grounds were clear and sparkling. I reached the gravesite I was in the habit of decorating every Christmas. Frost clung to the lettering, shielding the name. I pushed away the leaves and ice, working hard with my gloves, until a ray of sunlight illuminated the date of death: 1985.

It had been fifteen years. . . .

ONE

December 1985

We did not dare to breathe a prayer,
Or give our anguish scope.
Something was dead within each of us,
And what was dead was Hope.
—Oscar Wilde

The first big snowstorm of the winter of 1985 fell on Thanksgiving. After that, another massive storm seemed to enter the area every few weeks and drop inches, or even a foot, blanketing the landscape and making the town look like a Christmas card, long before the holiday arrived.

Schools were closed more times that winter than in the previous five years combined. Nearly every week, Doris Patterson finalized the lesson plan for her second-grade class, only to have to change it entirely due to yet another snow day.

After twenty-nine years of teaching, Doris was accustomed to the unexpected. Where some saw chaos, she saw opportunity. When the principal announced an early dismissal over the PA system, Doris tried to think up a fun, new assignment for her students, to accompany the traditional spelling and math homework. Assignments like *What are the flowers thinking beneath the snow?* or *When do birds make reservations to fly south?* Though simple assignments, she'd seen them stir her students' imaginations, creating wonderful memories for her scrapbook.

In the last couple of years, Doris had considered retiring but, for whatever reason, had always felt she wasn't ready. Until now. She'd recently informed the principal that this would be her last school year. Her husband had retired four years earlier from the post office. He was anxious to hit the wide-open roads with her in a brand-new RV he'd purchased, with "Herb and Doris" airbrushed in blue and pink on the spare-tire cover. Maybe it was all the snow there had been that year, but warm winters in the Southwest had begun to sound good to her.

Doris never showed favoritism outwardly, but every year there was one child in her classroom who captured her heart. In 1985 that child was Nathan Andrews. Nathan was quiet and introspective. He had sandy hair, huge blue eyes, and a shy smile. Doris noticed that his gentle nature was lacking the spark she'd seen in his previous two years at the school. While other students interrupted her with "Um, Mrs. Patterson, Charity just sneezed on my head" or "Hey, Mrs. Patterson, Jacob just hit me with a spitball," Nathan made his way to her desk without calling attention to himself and whispered, "Excuse me, Mrs. Patterson." He'd then wait patiently until she turned to him. Compared with the boisterous natures of the twenty-five other eight-year-olds in her class, Nathan's measured, serious disposition was, almost in a sad way, beyond his years.

Some of her colleagues maintained that children from poorer homes were harder to teach, had more disciplinary problems, and were generally mouthier than those students who came from middle- to upper-class homes. Doris disagreed. She knew Nathan's family could be considered lower income. Mr. Andrews worked at a local auto-repair shop and, people said, could barely make ends meet. Yet in all her years of teaching, Nathan was one of the most polite children she'd ever met. Doris had learned that it wasn't the size or cost of a home that created kind, well-adjusted children, but the love and attention that filled that home.

Nathan's mother had often volunteered at the school in the early fall. She had helped out in Doris's classroom, cutting out shapes and numbers for a math lesson, sounding out words for a student struggling with phonics, or stapling paper flowers and trees on the bulletin board. Nathan would beam with pride at the sight of his mother. But Doris hadn't seen Maggie Andrews in many weeks.

One day her husband, Jack, had come to school to tell Doris that his wife was seriously ill. Maggie Andrews had cancer, and the prognosis wasn't good. No wonder Nathan often seemed distracted. He was not old enough to fully understand the situation and probably didn't know that his mother was dying. But some days Doris could see it in the boy's eyes, a terrible sadness she recognized.

Her own mother had died of cancer when Doris was only twenty, and that single event had indelibly changed her. Her heart broke for the little boy as she watched him erase a hole into his paper, smoothing the tear with the back of his small hand as he continued with his work. She'd never had a student in her class who had lost a parent, and she found herself at a loss for words or actions. Somehow the gentle hug or extra playtime she'd given over the years to children who had lost a precious pet or extended family member seemed inadequate, even inappropriate. She still remembered that after her mother's death, she had wished that people would say nothing at all, rather than the trite, though well-meaning words they'd offered in sympathy. Sometimes being quiet is the greatest gift you can give someone, Doris thought, as she watched the boy sharpen his pencil, something terribly heartbreaking in the way he struggled to turn the handle. She whispered a silent prayer for God to draw near and wrap the little boy in His arms.

I slammed the phone down in my office. For the umpteenth time, I had tried to make a call, only to hear a busy signal in my ear. The day was short on hours, and I was feeling even shorter on patience.

"Would somebody tell me how these new phones

are supposed to work?" I shouted out my office door to my secretary.

Gwen Sturdivant, my assistant for the past ten years, hurried in to help me.

"First, make sure you select a line that isn't lit up," she explained.

"I know that, Gwen," I said, exasperated. "I'm thirty-eight years old. I'm familiar with the general uses of a telephone. I want to know why I hear that stupid busy signal every time I make a call."

"Once you dial, you need to wait for the tone and then punch in one of these codes for the client you're billing to." Gwen calmly demonstrated.

When I had started with the firm, the phone bill, along with the electric bill and office expenses, had been paid from the firm's general receipts. Now everything—the fax machine, the photocopier, the office phones—all had a code. As soon as someone could figure out how to program it, my pager would have a code too. Ordinary tasks like dialing the phone had been made more frustrating so the firm could bill our clients right down to the penny.

"Just get Doug Crenshaw on the phone for me!" I groaned.

I had been at Mathers, Williams & Hurst for thirteen years. Like many young attorneys, I had walked in the door a bright-eyed, naively optimistic law-school graduate. We were a small firm at the time, sixteen lawyers, but the location was perfect—only a few miles from my mother's home. My father had died of a heart attack five years earlier, and I wanted to move closer to my mother so I could keep an eye on her, in case she needed anything. My wife Kate's family lived only three hours away, so she couldn't have been more pleased when I took the job.

I spent the first day at MW&H in conference, a conference that had lasted thirteen years: conferences with clients, conferences with other associates, conferences with the firm's partners, conferences with secretaries, conferences with paralegals, conferences at lunch, conferences over the phone. The visions of wowing a courtroom with my verbal prowess faded as the firm's partners shifted many of their bankruptcy cases onto my desk. I had not minded the work at first. It was challenging and fun in the beginning, helping owners of small businesses and corporations liquidate their assets, seeing so many zeroes on a page reduced to one lone goose egg. Somehow my position within the firm as "the associate who helped with bankruptcy cases" changed over the years to "our bankruptcy associate." After I got over my initial disappointment and accepted that my dream of becoming a hotshot courtroom brawler was not going to play out (the bankruptcy cases that made it as far as the courtroom were invariably simple presentations of fact, never the in-your-face litigating tours de force I'd always dreamed of performing), I buried myself in the bankruptcy files to impress the partners. My position within the firm established, I concentrated on every young law student's goal: to become partner in just seven years.

I found that once I put my mind to a task and worked at it diligently, things came together as I had planned. Even with my wife, this seemed true.

I met Kate Abbott during my last year of law school. From the moment I saw her, I was smitten. She had recently moved into the neighborhood where I was sharing a small apartment with five roommates. My parents had paid for my books and tuition, on the condition that I support myself by taking on odd jobs to pay for food, rent, clothes, and whatever car I could afford. Meals in those days consisted of macaroni and cheese, Ramen noodles, and the rare special of Five Burgers for a Buck at the local Burger Castle. I owned one suit that my parents had bought me for my college graduation, three pairs of jeans, several ratty sweatshirts, two button-down shirts, a pair of loafers with a hole in the sole, and a pair of old running shoes. I would have felt my wardrobe was pathetic had not my roommates' clothes looked exactly the same.

I first saw Kate unloading boxes and secondhand furniture from the back of a U-Haul van. I set out to meet her, and then, once I met her, I set out to marry her. She was raven-haired and lovely. A certain melody filled the air when she laughed. We married a week after I finished law school.

Like most new law graduates, I was poor and saddled with debt. Kate continued her work in the marketing department of a small local hospital while I looked for a job. Though her salary was paltry, it paid the rent on our tiny one-bedroom apartment and put gas and the occasional spark plug in our beat up Plymouth Champ. We both knew we would struggle for a few years but that once my career took off, we'd live comfortably.

With my job secure at Mathers, Williams & Hurst, the money started rolling in. Kate suggested that we stay on in our apartment, or maybe move to a small condo for a few years, so we could sock away savings for our future. I disagreed; we couldn't entertain my colleagues in cramped quarters decorated with hand-me-down furniture from our parents or the Goodwill store. Like it or not, part of being an effective attorney is looking the part, and I felt that extended to our home.

We bought a large brick house in a respectable neighborhood and filled it with furniture. My old wardrobe was quickly replaced with freshly starched Polo shirts, Hart Schaffner and Marx suits, and Johnston and Murphy shoes. I considered the Plymouth Champ beneath Kate's status and sold it for $500, buying her what she called a "no-personality" used Volvo sedan, to sit beside my new BMW in our new two-car garage.

Both cars, like the home and the furniture, were financed. Kate had grown up in a home where nothing was purchased on credit. Her parents hadn't even owned a credit card until she was in college, and the card was used only for absolute necessities; the balance was paid off at the beginning of every month. As hard as she tried, Kate couldn't see as crucial to our well-being a Carver CD player, tape deck, amp, and preamp, a Thorens turntable, B&W speakers, hi-fi Mitsubishi VCR, or 27-inch Proton monitor. But I always prevailed. Each item was the best our money could buy, and I justified the purchases by reasoning "We have the money, and we're not tied down with kids yet. Let's have some fun with it while we can." When Kate complained that the house was too large, as she often did, I reminded her that we would need extra room after the children were born.

We were just about to celebrate our fifth wedding anniversary when Kate got pregnant. I had imagined that we would wait a couple more years to start a family. A few months into the pregnancy, I wanted to put the house on the market to move to a neighborhood with better schools.

"Robert, the baby won't be in school for years," Kate protested.

"Once the baby comes, we'll have twice as much stuff, and the move will be twice the headache," I said. "This is the right time."

We put our place on the market and began the search for a new house. Several of my colleagues lived in what was called the Adams Hill section of town, an older neighborhood that boasted of even older money. The area was named for Thomas Adams, one of the area's founding residents, who claimed to be related to President John Quincy Adams, though none of the locals had ever bothered to research his genealogy.

People of affluence and influence have lived in Adams Hill since before the turn of the twentieth century. The streets were lined with red maple and giant oak trees older than the oldest resident of Adams Hill. The lawns were professionally manicured; the shrubs were trimmed and clipped. The well-kept homes were all built of brick, wood, and stone, with not a panel of vinyl siding in sight. Great Victorian homes with enormous wraparound porches nestled among the oak trees, next to brick colonials with huge antebellum columns out front. Each home had a story. Many even had placards positioned next to the front door stating the year the home was built and any other information deemed worthy of sharing with those fortunate enough to ring the doorbell. Finding a residence that was actually for sale, as opposed to handed down from one generation to the next, was nearly impossible.

When the new listing popped up on our real-estate agent's computer, she couldn't reach for the phone quickly enough to call us. My palms began to sweat as I anticipated walking through what could be my dream home. Even Kate couldn't suppress a smile when the Realtor led us into the drive. The front was gray stone and yellow wood, with a beautiful double-tiered wraparound deck. It was a big house and, of course, that meant a big mortgage, but I wanted Kate to have lots of space to create a lovely home for our family. A home, like my mother's, that would come alive at Christmas with a roaring fire and a tall, sparkling tree.

Though the firm was pleased with my work, there were times I wished I'd opened a private practice, the way so many of my law-school buddies did, hiring two or three associates, their names painted in gold letters on doors (Gerald Greenlaw & Associates), on lawn signs, (Curtis Howard & Associates), or on parking-garage walls (Thomas Michelson & Associates). Instead of working eighty hours a week for someone else, I could have been working for myself—Robert Layton & Associates. It was too late to start over now, however, and our brand-new mortgage confirmed it. What I lost in freedom, I made up for in the security of working for a larger firm.

In the seventh year of my service with them, the partners at Mathers, Williams & Hurst unanimously made me a partner. They called me into the conference room, each partner seated in a leather chair at the cherry table that ran the length of the room. They made their announcement, clapped me on the back with congratulations, promised to get together with the wives very soon, and went back to work. The celebration lasted all of two minutes. I sat alone at the table as they filed out, thinking that this moment hadn't lived up to my expectations. Then I slowly walked back to my office, shut the door, and began sifting through the bankruptcy files Gwen had placed on my desk that morning.

I was so busy for the rest of the day that I completely forgot to call Kate and tell her the news. By the time I pulled into the driveway, the house was dark. Kate, in her seventh month of her second pregnancy, was no doubt exhausted chasing after our two-year-old daughter, Hannah. Like the first, this pregnancy was unplanned. To be honest, I had wanted to wait a few years before we had another child. I was so busy, I hardly had time to see Hannah. I worried that I would not be able to be a proper father to baby number two . . . and if I was, would it be at Hannah's expense?

Kate, of course, was ecstatic. Hannah had brought a joy into her life that I hadn't seen in a long time, and I knew this baby would do the same. Kate loved being a mother. I can admit that she was much more adept at being a mom than I was at being a dad. I had to work to understand what my daughter was saying, whereas Kate could carry on a full conversation with her without missing a beat.

I pushed open Hannah's door, her Winnie the Pooh night-light smiling at me from across the room. I walked softly to her bed. She looked so much like Kate when she was asleep, but when her eyes were open they blazed, as my mother said, with the same fire she'd seen in mine when I was young. I kissed her on the head, picking Bobo, her one-eyed stuffed bunny, off the floor, and put him back under the blankets before leaving the room. Peeking into our bedroom I saw that Kate was asleep. I heard her slight snoring, which had gotten louder as her pregnancy progressed, one of the side effects, as was fatigue, but even so, during the first pregnancy, she used to wait up for me. I closed the door and made my way down the stairs into the kitchen for something to eat.

In the refrigerator I found a cold, wrapped hamburger patty and some macaroni and cheese. As I put the plate in the microwave, I wondered when we would ever be able to eat food again that didn't come in colors, shapes, numbers, or that wasn't smothered in processed cheese. I'd come too far to be eating macaroni again, the way I did when I was single. Finding a hamburger bun or condiments was too much hassle, so when my food popped and splattered in the microwave, I took it out and let it cool as I poured myself a glass of milk. The recessed lighting I had had installed under the kitchen cabinets burned dimly as I sat down at the kitchen counter and toasted myself, "To Partner Layton," I said, raising the glass. And as the clock struck ten, I ate my rubbery hamburger and my macaroni and cheese, alone.

One night, shortly before Christmas, I came home to find the house dark, save a blue light glowing in the living-room window. Hannah, now eight, and her six-year-old sister, Lily, were long asleep. It was the third time that week I'd gotten home late, though the holiday season was always busy. Everyone was putting in eighty-hour weeks, and I couldn't expect special treatment. To top it off, Gwen had been crying in my office that morning. The long hours were "ripping her apart" and "wearing her down." She threatened to quit, as she had for the last eight holiday seasons, so I gave her the rest of the day off, with pay, knowing she would be back the next morning good as new and telling me how relieved she was to have gotten her shopping done.

I put the Mercedes in the garage, dropped my briefcase heavily on the dining-room table, and went to the living room, expecting to find Kate asleep in front of an *I Love Lucy* rerun. Instead, she was awake.

"Girls asleep?" I asked, flipping through the stack of bills.

"Yep."

"Everybody have a good day?" I asked, uninterested.

"Yeah. You?"

"Busy. You know. I let Gwen have the day off. Had her holiday cry," I said as I walked into the kitchen. I opened the refrigerator door and began my nightly rummaging for dinner leftovers.

Kate moved to the dining-room table and watched for a long time before she finally spoke.

"I'm tired, Robert," she said evenly.

"Go to bed. You didn't have to wait up for me," I told her halfheartedly.

"No, Robert. I'm tired of this. Of us."

I stood frozen, my head still in the refrigerator. In my heart, I'd known the marriage had been over for nearly a year, but I had never imagined either one of us would have the courage to bring it up. I should have known it would be Kate. She'd always been the stronger one. The year before she had accused me of having an affair. I wasn't. She never believed me, but there had never been another woman. Frankly, there'd never been enough time for Kate, let alone another woman. Some nights, I knew, I worked late because it was the one thing I knew I could do for my family, one concrete step I could take to make sure that they had the things that they needed, that the girls' college tuitions were taken care of, that there was a roof over their heads. Some nights I worked late because I didn't know what else to do, and because I didn't want to go home and face the fact that we were in trouble.

I dragged some sort of casserole from the top shelf of the refrigerator and silently pulled a plate down from the cabinet. I couldn't seem to find the words I wanted to say.

"I'm sorry, Robert, but I just can't do this anymore," Kate continued. "I can't go on pretending that everything's all right. It's not all right. It hasn't been for some time. Living under the same roof doesn't mean we're living together. I need more than this."

I stared blankly at the casserole in front of me. She needs more, I thought to myself. Well, I don't have any more. I have given everything, I reasoned. I can't work harder. I can't do more. But I didn't say any of that.

"Let's face it, you left this family a long time ago. We'll stay together through the holidays," Kate explained unemotionally. This all seemed too easy for her, almost as if she'd rehearsed it several times.

"I don't want to ruin my family's Christmas or your mother's, and it'd absolutely kill the girls if we split up right now. But as soon as the holidays are over, you'll have to find another place to live."

There. It was over. She paused briefly to see if I would respond in any way, but, as expected, I didn't, so she softly wandered back upstairs and closed the bedroom door.

TWO

The more I think it over, the more I feel that there is nothing more truly artistic than to love people.
—Vincent van Gogh

Doris Patterson loved dressing her classroom for Christmas. She and her giggling, excited students had cut out paper snowflakes and Christmas trees, snowmen and Santas, from brightly colored construction paper, then decorated them with glitter and cotton and yarn. She brought in a four-foot artificial tree to adorn with popcorn and cranberry strands, gingerbread men, and candy canes. Her students chattered loudly as they worked, until the room reached a raucous din with the anticipation of Christmas.

Doris always had her students prepare a Christmas wish list of the things they wanted Santa to bring

34

them, but this year, she had broken with tradition. She knew what Nathan would wish for. She couldn't ask him to stand up in front of his classmates to say out loud what he wanted so badly. She knew that Nathan would give back all the toys he'd ever received at Christmas if his mother could just get better. This year, Doris had asked her students to focus on their favorite Christmas memories and to write them into a story. She hoped the assignment would help Nathan concentrate on the happy times he'd shared with his mother, instead of the time that would never be.

When Nathan's father told her how sick Maggie was, Doris volunteered to drive the boy home from school each day. With all of the stops it made, the school bus took forty-five minutes to bring him to his driveway, and she could get there in fifteen.

"I can't have you do that, Mrs. Patterson," Jack said adamantly.

But Doris insisted. She remembered how she would have given anything for a few more moments with her mother. Other teachers felt Doris was going beyond the call of duty, but if driving five extra miles a day meant a little boy could spend thirty extra minutes with his mother, she would more than gladly make the trip.

The car ride was usually quiet. Doris didn't force conversation, although she often wondered what the child was thinking about. Perhaps his thoughts weren't sorrowful at all, but were instead of his mother being miraculously healed. Doris had had the same dreams when she was young—that God would simply touch her mother and destroy the disease that had viciously eaten away at her, yet there were times, she knew, that miracles didn't happen, that people didn't recover. Sometimes they never get better. In the silence of the car rides Doris would pray for her small passenger. For peace . . . for hope . . . for comfort.

Nathan slammed his teacher's car door and ran up the gravel drive to his home. The beginnings of a snowman stood in the yard, but whoever started it had quit, leaving a single large ball with stick arms and pinecone eyes and a soda bottle for a nose. Neither the driveway nor the sidewalks had been shoveled; foot-paths were beaten down in the snow. Today, Nathan and his mother were going to make Santa cookies for relatives and neighbors. Each year they worked for hours on the cookies, decorating them just right with food coloring and silver sugar balls before wrapping them and presenting them as gifts. He ran in the front door to find his grandma Evelyn preparing the butter and eggs and mixing bowls they were going to use. His mother lay propped on the hospital bed in the living room, smiling as he threw open the door.

"Are we making them?" he shouted.

"We're making them," Maggie laughed. "We've just been waiting for you!"

"Well, come on!" he said, tugging on the sleeve of her bathrobe.

"I'm watching Rachel right now," she said, indicating the playpen, "but I'll help in a minute."

Maggie's eyes filled with tears as she watched Nathan jump into the kitchen. She wasn't strong enough to help in a minute, and both she and her mother knew it.

Evelyn had moved in the previous Thursday, the same day Sylvia, the visiting hospice nurse, arrived and the medical-supplies truck delivered the hospital bed. Evelyn had been coming in every day, but Jack asked her if she could stay around the clock, explaining that Maggie no longer had the energy to take care of Rachel.

Evelyn was an active sixty-year-old widow, and the death of her husband four years earlier was easier for her to deal with than the impending death of her youngest child. It wasn't supposed to be this way. Parents were supposed to go first. It was the logical progression of life. Sometimes, when Evelyn was alone in the shower or in the car, she would weep until she was certain her heart would burst. She wept for her grandchildren, for Jack, for her beautiful daughter, and for the ache that was growing sharper with each passing day.

Maggie listened as her mother cracked the eggs into the cookie batter, each flourish producing a giggle from her son. Maggie loved to hear him laugh. Nathan had grown quiet during the last few months, though they hadn't yet told him of the severity of her illness. Evelyn craned her neck and winked at Maggie, then dabbed the end of Nathan's nose with the gooey concoction, causing a belly laugh that shook his small frame from head to toe. Rachel stretched herself to see over the playpen and laughed with delight. Maggie struggled to sit up, listening as her mother and Nathan cut out each cookie with precision. These were the last smells of Christmas, the last smiles of her little boy, the last squeals of her baby girl, that she would ever experience. She didn't want to commit them to memory, but, rather, she wanted to be fully present in the here and now, and love with all her soul.

Maggie had met Jack Andrews when she was twenty-three. Her new 1974 Ford Escort, her pride and joy, was making weird braking noises, so she took it into City Auto Service. A girl she worked with in the bakery at Ferguson's Supermarket recommended City Auto as an honest garage. A young man, wiping grease from his hands, came over as she drove into the shop. Maggie was immediately taken with his intensely blue eyes. She read the name stitched on his green overalls: Jack. A nice, hard-working name.

"What can we do for you?" he asked, and then smiled the most genuine smile she'd ever seen. Jack seldom took notice of the people who came in to drop off their cars for repairs. When the slender Maggie stepped out of her Escort, tucked her dark bobbed hair neatly behind her ears, and smiled, he was immediately interested in more than just her car.

"I think it's my brakes," she said.

"I do," she said six months later.

When Nathan was born, Maggie cut her hours at Ferguson's to part-time. She and Jack did not want to drop their kids at day care, for strangers to take care of them. If they couldn't rearrange their schedules so one of them could watch Nathan, they'd agreed that Maggie would quit working. It might mean that, on a single income, they'd never live in a big house on Adams Hill or afford better furniture, but it was worth the sacrifice to know that their child was being raised by his parents.

Nathan was two when Maggie and Jack moved into a small, aluminum-sided ranch house on 14th Street in a quiet neighborhood of older homes. The house needed some work. The roof leaked in what would be Nathan's bedroom, the subflooring was rotten where the sink leaked in the kitchen, there was termite damage in the foundation, the carpeting needed replacing throughout the entire house, and much of the plumbing was rusting and needed new copper pipes. The prospect of buying a home in such disrepair might have daunted other couples, but Jack was an all-around handyman, a true "Jack" of all trades, Maggie called him, and she loved helping him. She could rip up floorboards and subflooring as good as any man, or hold a flashlight lying on her stomach under the kitchen sink for hours without complaining as Jack twisted and yanked and soldered the pipes. She loved to watch Jack work, and working together on the house gave them hours of uninterrupted time together. Whereas other couples struggled to find something to talk about, Jack and Maggie never wanted for conversation. When friends wanted to go out after work, Jack went home, even though they teased him and told him he was getting soft, but if that was true he didn't mind. He enjoyed being with Maggie more than anything else in the world. He loved to come home and find out what new improvement she'd made in the house, which gradually they had transformed from the shabbiest dwelling on the block to the nicest.

Two large elm trees guarded the front of the house, and an oak and a maple stood in the back. Maggie thought they were the most beautiful trees she'd ever seen. All her life, she wanted to live in a home surrounded by enormous shade trees, and now her dream had come true. She began tearing up the earth around the bases of her shade trees and prepared the soil for what would be a circle of tulips or daffodils. She dug up the soil by the tiny front porch and planted creeping phlox by the sidewalk, dianthus around the shrubs, daylilies between the shrubs, shasta daisies and Victoria salvia near the house, and pansies to fill in the rest of the bed with splashes of purples, reds, and yellows. Each afternoon when Jack arrived home, she'd take him and Nathan by the hand and describe what flower she had planted where, and in which month it would bloom.

When Maggie discovered she was pregnant a second time, Jack's eyes welled with tears. At such moments, Maggie was humbled by the love she felt for her husband, overwhelmed that God had sent him to her. Maggie had gone back to the bakery part-time, once Nathan started kindergarten, but when the baby came, she would quit her job and stay home. Money would be tight, but they knew they could make it. Jack made a modest but honest living at City Auto Service, and he'd already been there five years. He'd be up for another raise soon, and that would help.

The owners of City Auto were three brothers—Carl, Mike, and Ted Shaver. The shop was originally called Three Brothers, until they decided that the name made it sound as if it was owned by the Mafia. They then changed the name to the more respectable City Auto Service. They were a small operation with two full-time employees—Jack in the shop and Jeannie in the office—and one part-timer who worked in the garage on Saturdays. Mike ran the business end of the shop (he was always the first to claim he couldn't charge a battery to save his life), and Carl and Ted both worked in the garage. The Shavers were good, decent men to work for, and in his time there, Jack had learned more from them than he ever had in school. They provided insurance for their full-time employees, and each Christmas they'd give a Butterball turkey and a fifty-dollar bonus.

When Jack tossed and turned at night, worrying about money, Maggie always told him, "There's a difference between needs and wants, and we have everything we need." When Jack's spirits sagged, wishing his wife could shop at department stores like other women she knew instead of at yard sales and thrift shops, Maggie would hold his face in her hands and say, "It doesn't matter, Jack. None of it matters. We're healthy. We're happy. All that other stuff is just extras. Maybe one day we'll have it, but right now, we don't need it." That was always enough to keep Jack going. Maggie reached his soul in a way no one else could.

Years earlier, he figured he'd probably live his life as a single man. Now, when he thought back to those days, he thanked God again and again for directing Maggie to City Auto Service.

During her second pregnancy, Maggie often felt as if her belly was bloated but passed it off as the woes of pregnancy. After the smallest of meals, she'd feel terribly full. It was so unlike her pregnancy with Nathan, when she'd craved everything in sight. After Rachel was born, Maggie noticed the discomfort again yet disregarded it as a postpartum side effect. She mentioned her problem to the pediatrician at Rachel's four-month follow-up visit. The doctor agreed it was probably associated with the pregnancy but suggested Maggie get it checked out. Another month went by before Maggie relented and made an appointment to see her gynecologist, who ran a series of tests and told her he wanted to see her again in another two weeks to go over the results.

Maggie arrived for her appointment with Rachel on her hip.

"I'm sorry," the receptionist said. "The doctor was

in the delivery room all morning, so he's behind schedule. Have a seat—it could be a while."

A woman dressed in a navy-blue tailored suit, carrying a rich Italian-leather briefcase, approached the appointment desk as Maggie sat down.

"I'm here to see Dr. Nylander," the woman in the blue suit said.

"He's with patients right now," the receptionist droned, barely lifting her eyes from her computer.

"I'll just wait for him then," the woman said, turning her attention to the nearly full waiting room.

"He's going to be a while," she replied in a pinched voice. "He's got three other patients ahead of you."

"That's okay," she said. "He's expecting me."

She spotted an empty seat next to Maggie. She slid into the chair and set the briefcase on her lap. Rachel made a loud gurgling noise that sounded like a sink backing up, then smiled.

The receptionist slid open her glass window: "Maggie Andrews."

"That was fast," Maggie exclaimed as she approached the desk.

"Mrs. Andrews," the receptionist continued. "Your insurance is only going to cover a portion of your tests, which means you will be responsible for the remainder of the charges," she said, handing her the printout of expenses.

"Do I have to pay them today?" Maggie asked, jiggling and shifting the baby.

"Charges are expected to be met on the day of service," the receptionist answered, typing feverishly into her computer.

Maggie scanned the bill and asked hesitantly, "Is there a way that we could be set up on a payment plan where we could pay off a little of the bill each month?"

"Services are supposed to be paid for on the day of service," the receptionist reiterated loudly enough for everyone in the waiting area to hear.

"I understand," Maggie whispered, "but it would be helpful if we could pay monthly on the bill."

"I'll see who I can talk to," the receptionist snapped, closing her window.

Embarrassed, Maggie sat back down in her seat, bouncing Rachel, who had begun to slightly whimper.

"She must have charmed her way into the job," the woman next to her said with a smile. "I work here, and I'd like to say she's just having a bad day, but if that's the case, I've unfortunately never caught her on a good one."

Maggie chuckled, relaxing, and said, "What do you do here?"

"Freelance marketing. I'm on a team that creates the annual reports, so we interview doctors and patients in each department and review the new medical equipment, look at procedures, and compile the report . . . I'm Kate," she said, extending her hand.

"Maggie Andrews."

Rachel hiccupped and squirmed on her mother's lap.

"She's beautiful," Kate said, admiring the infant's wide, bright eyes.

"She is when she's not mad," Maggie laughed.

"What's her name?" Kate asked.

"Rachel."

"Oh! I was going to have a Rachel," Kate gushed. "It was between Hannah and Rachel, and on the day she was born, I looked at her and decided on Hannah."

"I love that name," Maggie replied, smiling at the wriggling baby on her lap. "It's a beautiful name she can grow into."

"Exactly!" Kate exclaimed. "How old is she?"

"Five and a half months," Maggie answered sweetly. "And I have a seven-year-old in first grade. How about you?"

"Two girls," Kate smiled. "My youngest started kindergarten this year. I thought it would kill me," she laughed.

"When I put Nathan on the school bus for his first day in kindergarten, I cried the rest of the morning," Maggie agreed. "That's why I take this one with me wherever I go." Rachel whimpered and coughed before straightening her body into a full-blown crying jag.

"I'm so sorry." Maggie apologized, lifting the baby onto her shoulder. "She's had an upset stomach."

"I understand," Kate comforted. "Both of mine had colic."

"Did you want to have any more?" Maggie asked,

thumping the baby's back.

"Oh, I would have loved to. I don't think my husband would have loved it, though."

Maggie liked this stylish woman. She wasn't self-absorbed, the way she'd always assumed rich people would be. "What does your husband do?" Maggie asked, shushing the baby's cries.

"He's in law," Kate replied. There was an odd sadness in her voice. It made Maggie suddenly feel sorry for her.

"What does yours do?" Kate asked.

"He's a mechanic," she answered.

"Maggie Andrews," the nurse said, standing in the doorway.

"Oh, that's me, again," she said, patting Rachel's back.

"I can watch her if you'd like," Kate offered, smiling. "I can't see the doctor until he finishes with his patients anyway "

Maggie would never leave her baby with a complete stranger, regardless of how kind she thought she was. She looked uncomfortably toward the nurse waiting for her in the doorway. "I could never ask you to do that," Maggie said, inching toward the nurse.

"We can all vouch for Kate around here, Maggie," the nurse smiled. "She's been around here a long time. If you'd like, we can leave Rachel with her in Dr. Nylander's office while he sees you. Might make your appointment a little easier. It's up to you."

"Dr. Nylander wouldn't mind?" Maggie asked.

"Not a bit. He has to meet with Kate in his office anyway."

The look in the nurse's eyes told Maggie her baby would most definitely be safe. "Thank you so much," she said, feeling reassured, and handed the child to Kate.

"Not a problem," Kate cooed at the baby. "It's been way too long since I've held one this small."

Kate patted the baby's back and walked her into the doctor's office. She loved the flexibility of her job. It paid well, and she was able to drop Hannah and Lily off at school, work a few hours, and be done in time to pick them up. She was completely at ease interviewing doctors and medical experts from around the world and was thoroughly proficient writing about medical issues, technology, and the latest research findings. People found her sharp and engaging, always the consummate professional, which is why the hospital continued to hire her year after year. Kate continued to walk the baby around, bouncing, patting, and rubbing her until Rachel burped.

When she came out of the examining room, Maggie found Rachel asleep in Kate's arms. She weakly thanked her new friend.

"Oh, I loved it," Kate smiled. "Are you all right?"

"Thank you again," Maggie managed, sliding the baby bag over her shoulder.

"Good-bye, my little Gerber baby," Kate whispered, squeezing the child's tiny hand.

Maggie buried her face into Rachel's warm body,

kissing her belly, and left quickly. She heard Kate ask her if she wanted to go to the coffee shop and talk, but she didn't answer. Her visit to the doctor had left her stunned and shaken. Maggie had barely sat down in his office when he told her he'd sent her blood work for oncological testing. Several tests confirmed she had ovarian cancer.

"Do you know if your grandmother had it?" the doctor asked.

"No. Not that I know of."

"Anyone else in your family—aunt or a sister, per-haps?"

"No. No one."

He wanted to start aggressive treatments right away. The cancer had gone undetected for so long that he feared it had already spread more than they would have liked. He picked up the phone and scheduled her an appointment with a surgeon. In all likelihood, he continued, she would need a total abdominal hys-terectomy and two other procedures she'd never heard of before. He explained that the procedures would detect if the cancer had spread.

When she came home, Jack held Rachel in his arms as Maggie told him the news. He sat silent for several minutes, holding the baby close to him, listening to her tiny breaths, breathing in her milky-powdery smell. He squeezed her tight. She was as beautiful as her mother. Her face looked exactly like Maggie's. His heart pounded anxiously. Could this disease take her from him? Could he lose her?

"What did they say exactly?"

"They've scheduled surgery for Monday."

Jack could feel the pounding of his heart.

"Then they'll start chemotherapy right away."

"Did they say anything about any sort of prognosis?"

"No."

"Did they say if the chances were good with this type of cancer?"

"They didn't say."

Jack couldn't help thinking that if they didn't say it, the chances, then, were not good—not good at all.

Maggie opened her eyes and realized she'd drifted off, lost in memory. She strained to sit up, listening as her mother and Nathan chattered and worked in the kitchen. As Evelyn opened the oven door to bring out another batch of cookies, an aroma of vanilla wafted into the living room. Maggie shut her eyes. What she would give to be covered in flour right now, watching her son's eyes gleam as she pulled tray after tray of hot Santa cookies from the oven. She threw her arm over her face.

"Oh God, help me," she prayed. "I don't want to leave my children. I don't want to leave my babies." She could stand the pain of the disease, but the pain in her heart was nearly unbearable. Then Nathan ran to her, holding a tray full of freshly frosted Santas, and plopped them clumsily down onto her lap.

"Ooh, look at this. What a baker you are," Maggie

exclaimed. She wiped her eyes and hoped he hadn't seen her. Nathan moved excitedly to the head of her bed and expertly cranked it into a sitting position.

"Time for his beard," Nathan yelled, running back into the kitchen for a bowl full of coconut. Together they sprinkled coconut across the smiling Santas, pressing the white flakes into each beard, talking and laughing as they worked.

THREE

Man is born broken. He lives by mending.
The grace of God is glue.
—Eugene O'Neill

My mother, Ellen Layton, had thrown a tree-decorating party at Christmas for as long as I could remember. When my brother, Hugh, and I were small, the party would begin first thing on a Saturday morning. Mom would rouse us out of bed with the smells of bacon, and pancakes in the shape of snowmen. Then the entire family would load into the station wagon and head to Hurley's Farm—John Hurley was an old friend of my father's—for a trek deep into the woods. My father, Albert, wielded the ax, occasionally letting one of us take a careful whack at the prized tree. Even later, when he'd acquired a small, gasoline-powered chain saw, my father insisted that the Christmas tree be hewn by ax, an antique double-bladed tool passed down by my grandfather, because it was tradition. Once home, Dad and I positioned the tree while Mom and Hugh braved the cold attic for the abundance of Christmas ornaments and decorations Mom had collected over the years. Mom sang and danced with Dad to Bing Crosby's "White Christmas" while Hugh and I busily continued with the tree, pretending not to see our parents' silliness.

I cannot ever recall seeing my mother happier than she was on those tree-decorating days. A joy radiated from her, and even from my father, who routinely conked out at six-thirty every evening, after getting up at five every morning to go to work. The whole family would get caught up in Mom's ecstasy, and would sing and decorate until every last ornament had a limb to call home. After we were grown, and my father had died, Mom continued her tree-decorating parties with another widow in the neighborhood. Just because they were alone didn't mean they couldn't enjoy the beauty of Christmas. When the grandchildren came along, the parties regained some of their traditional momentum, with the exception that we'd buy a tree from a supermarket parking lot instead of cutting one down from Hurley's farm, which saved time, and besides, the trees were invariably fuller and more symmetrical than the scruffier wild trees my father used to drag home.

A few weeks before Christmas, Kate and I loaded the girls into the Mercedes and drove the short distance to my mother's house. Mom had lived in the same brick Tudor house for more than forty years, and even though she was sixty-eight and lived alone, she insisted on decorating the outside of her home as a winter wonderland. Garlands of holly and ivy draped over the doorway, and a huge evergreen wreath hung prominently in the center of the door and on each of the front windows, tied with wide red-velvet ribbons. Bright electric candles threw off a brilliant light in the center of each window. Strands of small twinkling lights wrapped each yew and juniper and evergreen shrub, as well as each tree in the front lawn that could be reached with a ladder. The bigger trees provided the backdrop for the Nativity scene, complete with lighting.

When we were little boys, Hugh and I helped my mother set up the Nativity. She had bought the hand-crafted Nativity years ago at a yard sale. Though my mother's home was filled with magnificent antiques, she always claimed the twenty-dollar Nativity was one of her most prized possessions. As kids, my brother and I saw the set as little more than a collection of large wooden dolls, but each year Mom would explain the meaning of the Nativity to us. "This is the most miraculous thing about Christ's life, boys," she'd say. "The most miraculous thing isn't that He rose from the grave. He's the Son of God—you'd expect God to be able to raise His own son from the grave.

Don't you think?" And we would eagerly nod our heads in agreement. "But that's not the most spectacular thing at all. What's spectacular and mind-boggling is that God would want to leave the beauty of heaven to come to live here as a man. And you'd think that since Jesus was the King of Kings that he'd at least be born in a castle somewhere, not in some dirty barn. That's what's amazing!" she'd exclaim, turning Joseph ever so slightly toward Mary. "That's why Christmas is so special. Jesus came as a baby to Bethlehem—a baby that would grow up to live as a servant, not as a king." Plugging in the floodlights that beamed over the back of the shepherds onto the baby in the manger, she'd continue, "That's the beauty and wonder of Christmas, and that's why we'll set up the Nativity for as long as we can—to remind us. Isn't it a nice reminder, boys?" And we'd earnestly nod our heads again.

Since my father died, Dalton Gregory, Mom's neighbor of twenty years, had helped haul, hang, and string the outdoor decorations. He also shoveled her walk and drive when it snowed, though she never asked him to, no small commitment in the winter of 1985. Dalton and his family were the first black family to move to the neighborhood, arriving in 1965, and when the moving trucks backed into the driveway, my mother stood ready to work, holding a platter full of sandwiches and chips. When they moved in, Dalton worked as a high school history teacher and his wife, Heddy, worked in the

53

intensive care unit of the hospital as a nurse. In 1976, Dalton was made superintendent of schools, and even though his job kept him busier than ever before, he still marked on his calendar the day he would help my mother decorate her house. Twenty years separated them, but Mom, Dalton, and Heddy were more than just neighbors. They were friends. Dalton was hunched over, stringing his own simple strand of lights along the porch rails, when I got out of the car.

"Merry Christmas, Dalton! The house is award-winning. As usual."

"It better be. Your mother about worked me to death out here in the freezing cold."

"Why do you do it every year, Dalton?"

"Because there are three things I'm afraid of in life: my mother, my wife, and your mother. And at Christmas, I reverse the order!"

My mother swung open the front door and shouted "Merry Christmas" loud enough to wake Heddy's patients in the ICU. Hannah and Lily ran to their grandmother, wrapping their tiny arms around her waist. "Here are my Christmas babies!" Mom cried, kissing and squeezing them until they pulled away, giggling. Walking to the edge of her driveway, she teased, "Where are your Christmas babies, Dalton?"

"Just give my kids time," he said wearily, shaking his head. "One day they'll figure out how to make babies and you won't be the only obnoxious grandparent in the neighborhood!"

"Maybe not, but I'll still hold the title of being the first!"

"The first and the loudest," he laughed.

"Are you and Heddy coming over for lunch tomorrow?" she asked, rocking Lily back and forth on the top of her feet.

"I didn't know we were invited."

"I just invited you!" she said.

"Then we're coming," he replied waving his arm to shoo her away.

Mom led her brood into the house, which was very much like a Christmas botanical garden, with poinsettias, holly, and a garland of pine boughs filling the huge foyer. As Kate and I entered through the heavy cherry door, Mom playfully pointed out the mistletoe hanging just above us. Trying to avoid any awkwardness, we clumsily kissed Mom on both sides of her face.

"Not me," Mom joked, pointing at the mistletoe. "You're supposed to kiss each other." But Kate and I were already taking off our coats, preparing for a day of decorating. Mom promptly slid my coat back on, sending me out with a handful of money for the tree.

"Ferguson's, on the other side of town, has the prettiest ones, but they're more expensive," she instructed. "Maybe you should try the Daly's lot first. The trees there are smaller, but they're priced better."

"Where do you want me to go, Mother?" I sighed.

"Better get it at Daly's. It's closer."

"I'll be back in a minute."

"No! Wait!" she screamed. "Go to Ferguson's. I can't stand the idea of a small tree at Christmas. Get a great big pretty one at Ferguson's."

"You're sure?"

She paused for a moment and thought over the advantages and disadvantages of each lot.

"Yes," she finally sputtered. "Get a big, beautiful one at Ferguson's."

As I closed the front door behind me, Mom led Kate, Hannah, and Lily to the attic to retrieve the decorations. As they unwrapped each ornament, Mom would say "Your grandfather gave this to me on our first Christmas together" or "Your father made this for me when he was your age." Downstairs, in the living room, the girls presented their grandmother with the ornaments they'd made with Kate's help. I'd come home the night they'd made them, asking Kate the next morning about the mess left on the dining-room table. Kate always knew I hated cluttered, messy rooms and I accused her of leaving things in disarray on purpose.

I think my mother sensed something was wrong between us from the moment we walked in the door, but she also knew that neither one of us would want to talk about it, so she made as much small talk as possible.

"What are you doing in school, Lily?" she asked our dark-haired six-year-old.

"Learning about bugs," she said, squirming. Tugging at her sweater, she claimed, "Itched like the dickens."

"Ew. I don't think I'd want to learn about bugs," Mom said, scrunching up her face.

"I don't either, but they make you, anyway." Lily shrugged.

"How's Robert's work, Kate?" The two women had always had a good relationship. Mom knew not to meddle, and Kate always appreciated her mother-in-law's "What-I-don't-know-isn't-my-business-anyway" approach to her marriage.

"It's the same. Busy," Kate replied, head deep in a box of decorations.

"Has Gwen had her Christmas cry yet?"

"I guess so," Kate laughed.

"Will he be taking any time off for the holidays?"

"Christmas Day," Kate answered, without looking at her. "I don't know if he has any others scheduled. You know how busy he is."

"Daddy says he has a stack of work this high on his desk," Hannah exclaimed, standing on tiptoes and holding her hand far above her head.

Mom would withhold judgment until later, but she intended to wring my arrogant, ambitious, and selfish neck when I got back.

Although she could easily afford someone to cook and clean for her, Mom absolutely refused to have someone do this. "Why would I want someone to clean my home when I could get it cleaner?" she'd say to me. My father's salary as an insurance executive had afforded the best of everything in the home and had kept Mom comfortable since his death. I often wondered if she insisted on doing her own chores because it kept her busy, and that kept her from missing my father so much.

The girls buzzed around the tree while the dinner cooked, and my mother handed out popcorn strings, ornaments, and tinsel. Everyone scattered their treasures on the tall, dark spruce, while Bing Crosby, Nat King Cole, and Ella Fitzgerald entertained. When the last of the tinsel was hung, Kate set the table for dinner, and Mom carried in the platter of pot roast surrounded by potatoes, carrots, and rings of onions. A steaming bowl of green beans was set out, along with gravy, broccoli salad, fresh rolls, and iced tea. I couldn't remember why, but my mother had always served pot roast on tree-decorating day, probably for no better reason than that it had been on sale at Daly's twenty-five years ago—not much to base a family tradition on, if you thought about it. We made small talk around the table, most of it focusing on the girls and school and dance classes. Hannah proudly told her grandmother that she was first understudy to Clara in The Nutcracker. I promised that next year she'd get the starring role. Kate said we'd be just as proud of her if she didn't get the lead. Mom played along with us, pretending that everything was okay. Despite the fact that I felt like a fraud inside, I was pleased I hadn't spoiled my mother's holiday tradition. As Lily swallowed her last bite of German chocolate cake, Kate stood and began to clear the table.

"Kate, I'll get those," Mom insisted.

"No, Mom. Let me wash up."

"No, not today. Take the girls into the living room and enjoy the tree. Play that game they've been begging us to play with them all day. Robert will help me."

Kate slipped away from the dining-room table, thankful, no doubt, that she wouldn't be cornered in the same room with me, and ushered Hannah and Lily into the living room.

I stacked the dirty dishes and carried them into the kitchen. Mom began to scrape what was left on the plates into the garbage disposal as I continued to bring in bowls and dishes from the table. Then she asked me point-blank, "What's going on with you and Kate?"

I looked at her, shocked, stunned even. "Going on?" I stammered, trying to act nonchalant. "Nothing's going on."

"Robert, how old do I look?" she asked loading the dishwasher.

"Is this where I say you don't look a day over forty-five?"

"How old do I look, Robert?" she said impatiently.

"Mother, what is the point of the question, because I know how old you are. You're sixty-eight."

"And in sixty-eight years, don't you think I've

picked up a little discernment? A smidge of perception?"

"We're in the middle of an argument," I sighed. "You remember what those are. You and dad had them. Every couple has them."

"I've seen you two argue before," she said, turning on the garbage disposal.

"Well, I don't know what to tell you, Mom," I answered sarcastically.

"Sit down, Robert."

"I'm helping you clean up."

"I don't want you to help. I want you to sit."

I sat at the kitchen table as my mother put on a pot of coffee. She continued to load the dishwasher as she confronted me. "I know Kate. She's been in this family for a long time now. I know when there's something more than an argument going on between you two."

I swished a Christmas card around on the table as I pondered how to tell her. This wasn't going to be easy. She loved Kate like a daughter. I knew my mother wouldn't naturally take my side in the matter. She was too honest for that. I'd have to tell her the truth and be done with it.

"The marriage is over, Mom," I said bluntly, staring at the Christmas card.

"Why?" she questioned, dumping leftover broccoli salad into a Pyrex dish.

Why? I didn't know why.

"I'm not sure."

"You're not sure of what?"

I knew my mother wasn't going to make this easy. "I'm not sure why the marriage is over."

"Well you're in it, so surely you must have some idea as to why it's over," she said, stacking Pyrex dishes full of leftover food into the refrigerator.

"Mom, I've done everything I can," I stammered. "I've worked hard. I've provided a good living. A great home. I've given Kate and the girls everything they could ever want, but it's never good enough." I paused, waiting for my mother to interject, but her back remained to me as she cleaned. "Over the last couple of years we've just kind of grown apart."

I sat and waited for her response. She pulled out a soft-scrubbing cleanser from beneath the sink and rubbed diligently at a stubborn stain on the countertop. She held her tongue and simply listened. I shifted uncomfortably in the silence. I almost wished she would just let me have it rather than leaving me hanging.

"We just have different interests," I continued awkwardly. "I guess when we first got married we were both on the same page, so to speak. We wanted the same things. Shared a lot of the same goals. But somehow over the years all that shifted. I don't know how. Same as it does for a lot of marriages, I guess."

She reached into a cabinet for two coffee cups and poured a cup, sitting it in front of me. She quietly poured herself a cup and sat across from me, staring into my eyes. She always told me I looked so much like my father around the eyes—I'm sure she wondered why I wasn't acting like him.

"If you had to pinpoint what the number-one problem of the marriage is, would you be able to do that?" she asked.

I thought for a moment. This really wasn't the conversation I wanted to be having right now. "Um . . ."

"You don't know what the number-one problem is?" she pressed. "Because I do."

I looked up at her. This was exactly the conversation I wanted to avoid. My mother was never one to beat around the bush. I couldn't even begin to recall the times in my youth that I heard "Do you know what your problem is?" as she would continue to lay bare everything before me. In the same way, I always knew that if I approached her with any problem, she would be honest and open with me. It was the only approach she knew.

"Your marriage isn't working because you're too selfish to live with," she stated matter-of-factly.

"Thanks for the cup of Christmas cheer, Mother," I said, toasting her with my coffee.

"You've grown apart? I get so sick of hearing floundering couples say they've grown apart! I always want to say, 'Well, dingbats—what have you done to try to stay together?' "

"We've tried everything, Mom."

"And what is everything? You come home at eight or nine o'clock at night. You work on weekends. What exactly have you done to keep the marriage together?"

It was funny. For as long as I had been a lawyer, no judge or opposing attorney had ever been able to fluster me the way my mother could. I shook my head, watching the dark liquid swirl and slosh up the sides of the cup in my hands.

"What, Robert? What have you personally contributed to the marriage to hold it together?"

"I don't know, Mom. How about I've provided Kate with everything she could ever want."

"You've never given her yourself."

"I've given her . . ."

"You've given her things," she interrupted. "Never yourself. There's a huge difference. You've tried to finance your happiness, and that doesn't work. Kate never wanted to live in a huge house or . . ."

"Mom, you've always lived in a huge house, and you're happy."

"Because your father made me happy," she said with sting. "I'd have lived in a shoe box with him. It had nothing to do with the house. Kate never asked you for a new BMW, or for a big house, or for expensive clothes, because those weren't things that she wanted."

"She never had to ask for them because I gave them to her before she asked," I said triumphantly.

"Exactly!" she agreed. "Because those were all things *you* wanted her to have. Giving Kate things was so much easier for you than ever giving one minute of yourself. Piling stuff in front of her and the kids was a great way to block them from you. Women don't want

63

stuff, Robert. They want your attention. Kids don't want things. They can only play with so many toys at one time. What they want is their daddy to pay attention to them and hold them and laugh with them. That's what everybody has ever wanted from the beginning of time!"

I looked around the kitchen, hoping my mother would finish soon.

"You said you have different interests now? How would you even know what Kate's interests or dreams are? Tell me—what are her dreams?"

"I don't know," I said. "The usual things, to have a healthy family, and see the girls finish school and . . ."

"Those are hopes," my mother said. "Everybody has them. I'm talking about dreams. What are they? What are Kate's dreams?" She waited. I didn't answer, because I couldn't. Whatever they were, they were Kate's dreams, her business—she was free to pursue them, just as I was free to pursue mine.

"You don't know, do you? You're never there long enough to ask her. Maybe it's your interests that have changed," she said slowly. "Maybe other women are a little more interesting these days."

I rolled my eyes and groaned.

"There is no other woman, Mother. There never has been. Why do women always assume there's another woman?"

"Maybe because a wife figures that if you're not seeking attention from her, then you must naturally be looking for it somewhere else."

This was really an area I did not want to talk about with my mother!

"Mom. Believe me on this. There has never been another woman. Never." Oh how I wished she would release me from this conversation. "Even if I wanted to, which I *don't,* I'm too busy to even think about taking on another woman in my life."

"You're right," she said, nodding her head. "I apologize. I should have put a little more thought into that. You're way too busy to have a mistress when work is your mistress."

I buried my face in my hands. "You are making my head hurt, Mother."

She ignored me and forged ahead. "Sexual conquests make some men feel more powerful," she said, as if reading from the latest *Ladies' Home Journal.*

"Mother, can we please stop talking about this?" I begged.

"But your conquests aren't made in bed." I put my head down on the table. "Your conquests are at work. You're only as good as your last victory—but the little victories at home never count—the first steps, the crayon drawings on the refrigerator door, the first visit from the Tooth Fairy. None of that matters to you. Those little moments—those simple everyday victories—don't mean anything to you, but they mean everything in the world to Kate." I buried my head into my arms, bringing my hands over the top of my head. Despite my attempts to quiet my mother, she continued anyway. "Those everyday successes are never enough for you. It's the wins at work that make you feel like a man, not the little girls who wrap their arms around your legs and call you Daddy. It's the power high at work that charges your batteries, not the power you have in helping mold and shape another person's life." She stopped, exasperated. Sighing heavily, she added, "I just don't think I understand how you could so easily give up those precious little babies for something that's never going to matter on your deathbed."

I looked at my watch. It felt as if her verbal lashing had gone on for hours. The thought that I was giving up easily was preposterous. I was merely trying to be realistic.

"Are you in a hurry?" she lovingly snipped.

"No, Mother, I was just checking to see if you beat the record for talking the longest without taking a breath."

She laughed and poured me another cup of coffee, slicing off another piece of German chocolate cake.

"I don't want that, Mom," I said, but it was no use.

"Dalton and Heddy won't be able to finish up all that cake. I need to get rid of it."

As she turned her back to pour more coffee into her cup, I picked up my fork and began to separate the sweet, gooey coconut icing from the rest of the cake. "Eat all of it, Robert. Not just the topping," she said, scolding, without looking. Resigned, I pushed the frosting back to the cake and took a bite.

"Things are a lot different now than when you were

married, Mom," I said with a mouth full of cake. "People go through more complicated things than they did back when you and Dad married."

"And what are those things?" she asked, interested. "Power? Prestige? Jockeying for top position on the corporate ladder?" Her brow raised and crinkled after each question, seeking a response from me. "Those things have been around for centuries," she stated with certainty. "There's nothing new under the sun—just the same mistakes made time and time again, but the thing is, we're actually getting worse at figuring out what those mistakes are. Why do you think your divorce-lawyer colleagues are so busy?"

I sipped the coffee and swallowed hard, looking at my mother. "Mom, at this point Kate and I are past the mending stage. Things have gone broken for so long that they would be too hard to fix now. I know that's not what you want to hear, but it's the truth. We were going to tell you after the holidays because we didn't want to spoil Christmas for you or for her parents."

"How very grown up of you," she offered acerbically.

"But I have thought about trying to fix things. I really have. The bottom line is, making the effort wouldn't be worth it because Kate doesn't love me anymore." Somehow those words hurt more than I expected. "I'm sorry, Mom, but it's true."

She set her cup down with a thump.

"Nonsense," she blurted. "I know Kate. I know women. I know she still loves you, but she doesn't feel loved, Robert. All she wants is to feel that you love and need her and can't live without her. You make her feel like you're living with her because you have to, not because you want to. Women want to feel cherished, and that they're the most important thing in your life. You've made Kate feel as if she's the third or fourth most important thing, and the girls don't feel anything at all. You're just some guy who pays the cable bill and wanders through the living room from time to time." Her voice softened. "But I know she loves you, Robert. I know it wouldn't take Kate long to remember why she fell in love with you in the first place, and if you'd give up some of the things you're holding tight in your claws, you'd remember why you fell in love with her."

"Sounds easy, doesn't it?" I mocked.

"No," she retorted, defensively. "As a matter of fact, it doesn't sound easy at all. That's why divorce is sky-rocketing—because it's much easier than actually working at the marriage. But there isn't a book any-where that says marriage is easy." Her eyes blazed. "Never in the history of marriage ceremonies has any minister ever said, 'You may kiss the bride and be on your way to an easy life.' Whoever said 'Life's a breeze' should be smacked! That person didn't have a clue. Life isn't easy. Just when you get close to having it figured out, they haul you away in a hearse."

I leaned back in the chair, interlocking my fingers on top of my head. "Things sure did seem a lot easier for you and Dad."

She burst into laughter. "Oh, my goodness. Your father and I were like Ralph Kramden and Lucy Ricardo the first ten years of our marriage. He always wanted his way, and I always wanted mine, and we'd roll up our sleeves, jump into the ring, and duke it out till one of us got tired," she laughed. "If one person in a marriage expects to always get his or her way, they're going to be mighty disappointed."

"Ralph Kramden and Lucy Ricardo weren't even on the same show," I said.

"Exactly!"

"But you always worked things out. Kate and I have never been able to do that." I looked deep into the empty coffee cup. "When Dad died, you didn't have any regrets."

She thought for a moment and then scooted her chair away from the table. "Come with me," she motioned.

I followed as she led me upstairs and into the bedroom she'd shared with my father for over thirty years. She removed the hand-stitched quilt from atop the cedar chest her mother had given them on their wedding day and opened the cherry lid, the familiar piney fragrance I remembered from childhood filling the room. Rummaging through the chest, she lifted out a small box and opened the lid. She folded open the tissue paper and pulled out a long, straight-stemmed pipe made of burly briar and handed it to me.

"What's this?" I asked.

"This is my regret," she answered softly. "This is a

Dunhill Billiard from England. Your father always wanted one. I was saving it for a special occasion." She took it back from me. "You know what I thought about as I held your father's hand when he lay dying in that coma after his heart attack? I thought about this Dunhill Billiard pipe, buried up here in this stupid chest." She stared at it for a moment and then rewrapped the pipe in the tissue paper. "I don't know what sort of occasion I was waiting for," she said quietly, her voice trailing off, "because every day was a special occasion with your father. Every single day." She tucked the box back into the chest and closed the lid. Taking my hands, she pulled me down on top of it, sitting next to me.

"Don't treat your wife or your kids like they're not special, Robert," she whispered, her eyes glistening. "They should be the most special people in the world to you."

"I know, Mom," I said squeezing her arm.

"No. You don't. Maybe once you've lost them, you will. But don't lose them Robert." She grabbed my face and spoke plainly to me, "You and Kate can still make it," she said sincerely. "It's still fixable. But you have to work on fixing yourself first. It's too easy to want to fix someone else but the hard part is fixing yourself. Instead of demanding more from her, you need to give more of yourself." She dropped her hands and folded them around mine. "No man ever really lives, Robert," she said softly, "until he gives himself away to others. That's what you need to do. What did

I always tell you and your brother at Christmas?"

I rolled it off my tongue as if on tape. "That that's why Jesus was born in a manger. He humbled Himself to give His life away for mankind. That's the meaning of Christmas." I then spoke in a high voice to imitate my mother, "Isn't that right, boys?"

She laughed and smacked my leg. "Finally, you've remembered something I've said over the years. Now why don't you ever put any of that good advice to practice?"

She turned off the lights in her bedroom and was heading back to the kitchen when Lily greeted us on the stairs. "Grandma, I need a treat," she giggled. My mother raced her downstairs and cut slices of cake for everyone except me. (I just couldn't stomach the thought of one more piece.) She poured milk into tall Santa glasses for the girls and sat down at the table with them for the final snack of the day. When they finished eating, Mom took one more picture of Hannah and Lily by the tree, and then it was time for everyone to gather up their coats and hats and mittens, the great swishing of Gore-Tex and nylon ending with hugs at the front door. It was snowing again. Three inches had collected on top of the car since dinner. My mother told me to drive carefully and to call and let her know we were safe.

She went back to the kitchen and finished washing the dishes. She wrapped the leftover cake for Dalton and Heddy. Then, shutting off all the lights in the kitchen and living room, my mother fell into her

favorite winged chair, the one she and my father purchased years ago at an auction, and stared into the
lights of the uneven, magnificent mess of a Christmas
tree her granddaughters had decorated, and closed her
eyes. A few minutes later, the phone rang once, my
signal that we were home safely. Only then could she
fall asleep.

FOUR

Life must be lived forwards, but it can be
understood only backwards.
—Sören Kierkegaard

Monday was a day when nothing was going my way.
I had scheduled an early meeting with one of my more
important clients and was rushing out the door when
Kate reminded me I'd promised to drop Hannah off at
school that morning. Kate had to be at the hospital by
eight and had asked me last week to take Hannah. I'd
completely forgotten.

With traffic, I'd kept my client waiting for twenty-
five minutes. He was none too pleased. As if that
weren't bad enough, I'd recently taken my car in to
have the brakes worked on. Gwen had recommended
a place on the edge of town that was supposed to do
good work, and they'd quite cheerily told me to bring

the car back if there were any problems. The car was running fine, but I'd just received the bill. Now, I had a problem, and they were going to hear about it. You drive an expensive car and people think you have money to burn. They assume you won't notice if they pad the bill. On my lunch hour, I headed to the shop. I had better things to do with my time. I asked the receptionist if I could speak to whoever had worked on my car. She summoned a man with the name Jack embroidered on his overalls.

"Jack," the receptionist began, "this is Robert Layton, and he has some questions about the work done on his car."

"Thank you, Jeannie. What can I help you with, Mr. Layton?" Jack asked politely. By the look on my face, he appeared to be dreading the answer.

"Did you work on my car . . . Jack, is it?"

"Yes. Jack. I worked on your car along with Carl."

"Who's Carl?" I snipped.

"He's one of the owners. He's been doing Mercedes work for over twenty years."

"Well, you'd think he'd know how to fix them then, wouldn't you, Jack?" Jack winced every time I said his name. I was having a bad day, but, I reasoned, I pay good money for service, and I will make sure I get it. I won't let anyone take me for a ride.

"If your car still isn't running right, Mr. Layton, we'd be glad to fix it for you."

"By looking at this bill, Jack, I don't think I can afford to have you guys fix it again." I threw the bill on the counter. Jeannie turned her head to her desk, looking as if she wished the phone would ring. "Do you mind explaining this bill?"

Jack carefully looked over the work done and all the specific charges. "Mr. Layton, everything seems to be in order here."

"Everything seems to be in order, Jack?" I mocked. "Look at the total!"

"Our prices have always been below our competitors'," Jack assured me.

"Below your competitors'?" I said, amazed, reading from the bill. "Two hundred and seventy dollars for front-brake work? You're telling me that's below your competitors prices? I should have just taken it to the dealership."

Jack shifted from one foot to the other as Jeannie began rummaging through her desk drawers.

"You had warped discs on both front sides," Jack explained. "We took the old ones off, cleaned everything up inside, and then put on brand-new rotors. Sometimes we can just rotate the rotors, but yours were too warped to do that. We even rotated and balanced your tires at no charge."

"Oh, well," I said, throwing my arms in the air. "If I'd known you'd done that, I never would have complained."

Jeannie dug deeper into a drawer as Jack took a deep breath before attempting once again to appease me. "If your car's still shaking when you brake, you can leave it with us and we'll look at it again."

"No, thanks," I said sharply, yanking the bill away from him. "Like I said, I can't afford to leave my car here anymore. I guess since it's Christmas, you guys think you can jack up the prices on guys like me . . . no pun intended, Jack." Throwing open the office door, I added, "Oh, Jack, be sure to tell Carl that he shouldn't expect my business anymore," and slammed the door behind me.

Sylvia was checking Maggie's vital signs and gently caressing the thin arm resting on the bed. She glanced at the picture of Maggie up on the mantel and silently compared the image to the frail, gaunt shell of a woman lying before her. She changed the IV drip that administered medication through Maggie's arm and gently massaged her hands and feet. That wasn't part of her job description, but Sylvia felt that in more ways than one, tender touches were the most important part of her work. The redheaded nurse was ten or fifteen years Maggie's senior and had a sweet, sensitive spirit. Maggie liked her very much.

"Thank you, Sylvia," Maggie said, smiling. Sylvia had seen some of her patients fight the dying process all the way to the end, kicking and screaming until the sheet was pulled over their heads. Then there were others who somehow managed to face death without fear, despite the sorrow they felt for those they would leave behind, people who could somehow meet death with a strange confidence . . . a knowing. People like Maggie.

"You're welcome, baby. You feeling all right?" But Sylvia already knew what Maggie would say.

"I feel good."

Sylvia had seen other ovarian-cancer patients die, and she knew they didn't feel well.

"You're not lying to me, are you?" she teased. "Because Sylvia does not like to be lied to."

"I'm all right. Really."

"Oh," Sylvia exclaimed, running to the sofa. "I nearly forgot. I found this tucked away in one of my drawers last night," she said, pulling a beautiful red and green scarf from her purse. "The colors of Christmas." She pulled the blue scarf off Maggie's bald head and tied the new one on, fashioning it into a knot so the tails hung down her neck. "Oh, my. This one makes your eyes pop. Let me get you the mirror."

"Thank you, Sylvia," Maggie said. She smiled as she examined her image in the glass. "Last night I dreamed I had hair."

"You did?" Sylvia laughed. This wasn't the first time a patient had dreamed of having hair.

"And this time it was long and red, just like yours," Maggie said. Sylvia chuckled, adjusting the pillows behind Maggie's head. "I was driving a convertible, and my long red hair was blowing in the wind." Maggie stopped, realizing she would never have long hair again, knowing she would never get behind the wheel of a convertible. Sylvia brushed her cheek and squeezed her hand.

Rachel toddled to the bed and reached for her mother.

"Up," she ordered Sylvia.

The little girl would often want to get up into the bed with her mother to snuggle. Maggie would scratch her back or tickle her arms. When Evelyn first realized Rachel wanted to be in the bed with her mother, she worried that the child would squirm too much and somehow hurt Maggie. When Sylvia set up the IV drip, Evelyn worried Rachel might rip the needle from Maggie's arm. Evelyn tried several ways to discourage the baby from wanting to climb into the bed, but she would only persist, "Up," she'd scold, her little fists thumping her chubby thighs. Maggie would say, "It's all right, Mom. Set her up here," and Rachel would burrow close to her mother, never fidgeting for a moment.

"All right, baby girl," Sylvia said lifting the child onto the bed. "Get up there and love on your mama." Maggie wrapped her arms around Rachel, proceeding with the story of Cinderella and her handsome prince.

Sylvia marked some things on Maggie's chart, tucking it under her arm as she gathered her things to leave. "I'll be back tomorrow," she told Evelyn.

"Thank you, Sylvia," Evelyn replied, showing her to the door.

"I'll see you tomorrow, Maggie," Sylvia yelled. "And you too, Little Miss Rachel!"

Evelyn closed the door behind Sylvia, wishing that

they wouldn't see her tomorrow or the next day or the next, because her frequent visits meant Maggie was getting sicker and sicker. One day Evelyn wouldn't be able to care for her alone during the day, and Sylvia would be brought in for long shifts to help with Maggie's medications, bathe her, and take her to the bathroom. Evelyn pushed such thoughts out of her head and busied herself cleaning the bathroom. Through the open door, she listened to Maggie tell one story after another to Rachel, her enraptured audience. As each tale ended, Rachel would touch her mother's face and say, "More Mama," and Maggie would launch into Snow White or Rudolph or Joseph and Mary, each story more intriguing than the last. Rachel sat up in the bed when she heard her daddy's car in the driveway.

Jack had started going home on his lunch break as soon as Maggie told him she was ill. By the time he got home, ate, and went back to work, it was usually longer than an hour, but Carl, Ted, and Mike had all told him he should eat lunch at home, and if it took an hour and a half or two hours, it wasn't a problem. Back when City Auto first opened, a large part of its winter business was putting snow tires on people's cars, but now that everyone was driving four-wheel-drive vehicles, there was less of that. He was grateful for the extra hours at home.

Jack was untying his boots in the front hall when Rachel called out, "Daddy!" from the bed where she was lying next to her mother. Jack lifted her up from the bed as she reached for him, kissing her forehead. He sat her down and leaned over to kiss Maggie. "How do you feel?"

"Good. Not bad at all."

Evelyn emerged from the bathroom, whisking Rachel into her arms. "Who wants lunch?" she announced.

"Me!" the little girl shouted, pointing to her chest.

Evelyn set Rachel down, donned a pair of oven mitts, and took out the meat loaf she had been keeping warm in the oven. She put thick slabs of meat loaf between two slices of wheat bread spread with mustard, placed two large spoonfuls of potato salad beside the sandwich, poured a glass of iced tea, and handed it to Jack on the sofa. Evelyn managed to get a few bites of leftover mashed potatoes and applesauce into Rachel before laying her down for her nap, something Rachel always objected to vehemently.

"She always fights a nap," Evelyn sighed once the child was down. "Wonder who she gets that from?" she said, eyeballing Maggie. When Maggie was Rachel's age, Evelyn would practically have to tie her down for her naps. Humming, Evelyn had started cleaning up what little mess there was in the kitchen when Maggie called for her.

"Mom, what are you doing?"

"Just cleaning up a little."

"Could you come here for a second?"

Evelyn threw down the dishcloth, dashing into the living room. She had learned to act quickly over the last several weeks. Sometimes the pain left Maggie curled into a ball, begging for medication, but that was usually before one of Sylvia's visits, not after.

"What is it?" she asked.

"I just want to talk to both of you while we're alone."

Evelyn sat next to Jack, and they looked uneasily at Maggie.

"I have something very important that I want both of you to hear," she began.

Jack set aside his lunch and stood up to be closer to his wife's side. "What is it, Maggie?"

"As I was telling Rachel stories today this popped into my head, and I knew you'd both have to hear it because if just one of you heard it, you'd tell the other one someday that I never said any such thing."

"Well, what is it?" Evelyn asked, sitting up.

"I don't ever want you to force Rachel to wear my wedding gown."

Jack and Evelyn looked at each other.

"What?" Jack asked.

"I don't want you to force Rachel to wear my wedding gown."

"You got me all upset inside for that?" Evelyn protested.

"Yes!" Maggie laughed. "It's important to me. Twenty-two years from now, I don't want either one of you forcing her to wear my gown out of sympathy. She may not like that gown, and I don't want her to wear it just to make one of you happy. I want her to wear what will make her happy on her wedding day. Now, promise me."

"I promise," Jack chuckled.

"Mom?"

Evelyn crossed her arms. She could barely think of Maggie's death, let alone talk about it. And she would never consider laughing about it.

"You know, I don't like talking about these things," Evelyn said. "I may not even be around when Rachel gets married."

"Well, I know I won't be around, and that's why I want to make sure one of you two won't be forcing her to wear some old, ratty gown from the seventies."

"Fine! I won't make her wear it. You didn't wear mine—why would I expect her to wear yours?"

"Well, I'm glad we got that cleared up." Maggie laughed, noticing her mother had found no amusement in the conversation at all.

"For a minute there, I thought I was going to have to break you two up," Jack said, taking his plate into the kitchen. He didn't like to laugh about these things either, but if making light of them helped Maggie, then he was going to try his best to find the lighter side as well.

Maggie observed that her mother was obviously bothered by something. Evelyn stood up to follow Jack into the kitchen when Maggie stopped her.

"Mom, wait," she begged. "I didn't know that would upset you."

Evelyn patted her daughter's hand.

"I'm not upset. I just want to make sure Jack's had enough to eat." She attempted to make her getaway again.

"Mom, come on. Look at me. I can't chase you down. What's wrong?"

Evelyn sighed, trying her best to maintain control.

"It's just one of those things that I never imagined I'd ever have to think about," she said slowly. "I wish that Rachel would wear your dress. I wish that she'd want to wear it." Evelyn felt her emotions swelling, but she held them back. Jack leaned on the stove. This was a moment he knew would come, but he was not prepared for talking about the reality of Maggie not being with them for track races or football games, cheerleading tryouts or senior proms, graduations or wedding days. He braced himself as he walked into the living room and sat on the chair next to Maggie.

"Listen," Maggie started, looking at Jack and her mother. "We all know that Rachel's too young to remember me." A tear rolled slowly down Evelyn's face. "It's true, Mom. She is. But my things aren't going to make me alive to her. I want her to know things about my personality. I want her to know why I fell in love with her daddy. I want her to know that I would nearly burst into tears when I'd carry her through Ferguson's and people would stop me and say what a beautiful baby she was. And I want her to know that I thanked God every single day of her life for her. Those are the things I want to be kept alive in Rachel."

Jack stared at the floor, wondering if there would ever be an easy conversation in his life again.

"Can you do that for me, Mom? Can you keep me alive that way?"

Evelyn wiped her face and nodded.

"I can do that," she said convincingly. "I would love to do that." Yet there was nothing inside of Evelyn that would ever want to talk about her daughter in the past tense. She wanted to wrap her in her arms as she did when Maggie was the child who pleaded "Up. . . . Up" and simply make it all better.

Six inches of snow fell the last week of school before Christmas break. Doris had learned over the years that there was no point in expecting her students to concentrate on anything when the holidays loomed tantalizingly near. As red- and green-frosted cupcakes were passed out, Doris asked the students to stand and each read their story of their favorite Christmas memory.

Joshua told the story of making the biggest snowman on his block, and how some crazy neighbor came over in the middle of the night and knocked its head off, smashing it into a bazillion snowy pieces and making his little sister cry for three whole days. Alyssa related a tale about the year she got a brand-new puppy and how it went potty on her mother's brand-new sofa. Visiting Santa's workshop was Patrick's favorite memory. He got to see how all the toys were made and loaded into Santa's sled. He even got to pet a reindeer, which, he announced to the class, smelled like doo-doo, and that produced a chorus of giggles from the audience of eight-year-olds. Desmond loved visiting his Grandma and Grandpa, and eating fudge till he got sick. Tyler liked the year he stayed awake until four in the morning and caught Santa sneaking in through the kitchen door instead of coming down the chimney. He even claimed he'd taken a picture with his camera but couldn't find it to show the class. Of course, everyone was terribly disappointed. Nathan read a short tale about going sledding with his mom and dad, and then eating chicken and dumplings while his mom and dad danced around the house. When he was done, he quietly took his seat, licking the remainder of red frosting from the crinkled paper cupcake wrapper. Doris laughed and clapped after each student finished. Then it was her turn.

She recalled when she was also a child of eight, and on Christmas, her grandmother gave her a pair of shoes adorned with sparkly, pink beads. She put them on and twirled and curtsied and danced around the house, she said, feeling like a beautiful fairy princess until she fell asleep on her grandfather's lap. When she woke up the next morning, she was in her own bed . . . but was still wearing her beaded shoes. "So I got out of bed and danced and twirled and curtsied some more!" she exclaimed, as her students giggled. "I had never felt so special in all my life."

She led her students in choruses of "Jingle Bells," "Frosty the Snowman," and "Rudolph the Red-Nosed Reindeer," even popping in Rudolph's famous story in the VCR for a last-day-of-class treat. At the end of the day the students screamed in frenzied joy as they scurried to their locker cubbies at the back of the classroom to gather the things they'd crammed inside when they had arrived. Doris helped bundle them into their snow jackets, hats, scarves, boots, and gloves, each child looking like a plump, colorful goose when fully dressed. As the children embarked onto buses and into the waiting cars of parents, Doris couldn't remember having more fun with one of her classes. There was an electricity, a joy, that buzzed through the classroom unlike any Doris had experienced before. Maybe it was because it was her last year of teaching and she was letting go. Or maybe it was because God had filled the room with incredible laughter and song to help one of His smallest children through the greatest sadness of his life.

Whatever the reason, Doris was grateful. It had been a wonderful day.

FIVE

Faith is not intelligent understanding, faith is deliberate commitment to a Person where I see no way.
—Oswald Chambers

Jack had been installing a carburetor he'd rebuilt when Carl and Ted approached him.

"How's everything going, Jack," Ted began, sliding his hands in his pockets.

"Almost finished here, Ted. What d'ya need?"

"Nothing," Carl answered, folding his hands across his wide belly, then opting for his pockets as well. "We just wanted to let you know that we've talked about it and would like you to take as much time as you need right now." Carl scratched his bald head, slipped his hand back into his pocket, and continued, "Ted's son is back from college and can help us out here until he heads back to school in January. It'll do him good to get his hands dirty after all that readin'." When Carl said "we've talked about it," he meant he and his brothers.

Jack stared into the engine, trying to think of the right thing to say. Every now and then in life there were those people who couldn't take away the load you carry but they sure could make it easier. In their own quiet way, the Shaver brothers were making his load easier.

"I'll make up the work," Jack said to the carburetor, feeling too awkward to make eye contact.

"We know you would," Carl replied, talking to the same carburetor. "But there's no need to do that."

"You don't have to come into the shop to pick up your check," Ted added. "Mike will send it to you every week."

Jack fumbled for words. He would be receiving a check for work he wouldn't be doing.

"Now let me take over that carburetor," Ted said, stepping in beside him, "and you head on home."

Jack tried to speak, but Ted already had his head under the hood, and Carl had quietly disappeared. Jack washed his hands, grabbed his coat, and drove home for the last holiday season he would spend with his wife.

When Nathan arrived home, he was surprised to see his father there so early. Nathan showered his family with chocolate snowmen and hard-candy snowflakes. He hung a construction-paper Christmas tree at the foot of his mother's bed and lined the bed rails with the snowflakes he had cut out with his class that morning, using a roll of Scotch tape he got from the kitchen table, where Evelyn had started wrapping presents. When he stuck a crisp, white crafted paper snowflake onto the bed, Rachel ripped it off, laughing merrily at her crime.

"Rachel. No!" Nathan screamed, grabbing the torn

snowflake from his sister's sticky clutch. "Leave those alone." Rachel ran to the other side, ripped off another flake, and giggled endlessly as her brother fumed and hollered.

"You're ruining them," he yelled, pushing her down. "Stop it."

Jack picked up his crying daughter and turned her upside down, which led to shrieks of delight.

"That's enough, Nathan," Jack scolded.

"She was ruining them!" Nathan shouted.

"Well, now it looks perfect," Maggie affirmed. "I feel like I've been plopped down right in the middle of a winter wonderland."

Evelyn looked at her watch and scooted Nathan and Rachel out the door to go grocery shopping with her. She knew Sylvia would be there soon to administer some much needed pain medication. Maggie's pain had grown worse over the last several days, and she didn't want the children to see her in discomfort. The children never seemed to catch on, and if they complained about going somewhere, Jack would merely say, "But who's going to help your grandma if you don't go?" and Nathan would scurry to put his boots on as Rachel tumbled after.

When the dinner dishes were washed and put away, Jack helped Maggie into the bathroom. There were times nausea from the medications overwhelmed her, and after hours of queasiness she would finally vomit, which left her even weaker than before. She had motioned to Jack that she was not feeling well in the sign language they had developed between the two of them. He swung her legs over the side of the bed and eased her onto the floor. She'd lost a lot of strength, but she was still able to walk if Jack helped her. Turning on the fan, Jack supported her body as Maggie retched into the sink. He wrapped his arm around his wife, rinsed out the sink, and helped her back, gently tucking her into bed. With Jack's arm around her, Maggie felt as if he was the strongest man she'd ever known.

When Maggie was comfortable in her bed again, the family sat down together to watch *A Charlie Brown Christmas* before Evelyn laid Rachel down for the night. They laughed as the whole Peanuts gang prepared for the Christmas pageant Charlie Brown was directing. Rachel laughed particularly loudly while watching Snoopy dance with his nose sticking straight up in the air.

"That's one of my favorite Christmas stories," Evelyn said, scooping Rachel up in her arms. Nathan bolted upright, realizing he'd left his very own Christmas story in his backpack. Evelyn ran water in the bathtub for Rachel's bath as Nathan plopped down in the seat by his mother to read her his favorite Christmas memory.

"Mrs. Patterson had everybody stand up in class and read their stories," Nathan eagerly told his parents. "Tyler took a picture of Santa coming in his kitchen door, and somebody hacked Joshua's snowman to death."

"Oh, that sounds awful," Maggie said, smiling.

Nathan read from his paper: "My favorite Christmas memory was when my mom and dad and me went sledding all day long at Whitman's Farm. My dad fell off the back of the sled because we had too many people on it, and my mom laughed the whole way down the hill. Then we ate chicken and dumplings and drank hot chocolate, and my mom and dad danced around the Christmas tree." Maggie admired the story and smiled at the backward *d*'s, the *g*'s that looked like *j*'s, and the *m*'s with one too many humps. She complimented Nathan for having such a good memory. It was hard to believe that it had been only three years ago. Maggie could see it all as if it had just happened yesterday. She and Jack had sandwiched Nathan on the sled, and just a quarter of the way down the hill, Jack fell off and Maggie howled with laughter, watching him tumble and roll down the hill before coming to a complete halt, spread-eagle on his belly.

"That would definitely have to be my favorite Christmas memory too," she said, holding the story.

"Mine too," Jack offered. "Even though I couldn't walk straight for two weeks afterward."

"Then remember you and Daddy dancing around the tree?" Nathan teased.

Maggie's eyes blurred. Jack always loved to dance, even though he wasn't very good, but what he lacked in grace, he made up for in reckless abandon.

"Your mother is a fabulous dancer," Jack told his son.

"Mrs. Patterson told us her Christmas story about how she danced in a special pair of pink shoes her grandma gave her. She even slept in them," Nathan exclaimed.

"Oh my, they do sound very special," Maggie agreed, smiling.

Evelyn pulled Rachel from the tub and wrapped her in her favorite snuggly towel, then took her into her room, closing the door behind them. Maggie looked at her son's handsome face. He was his father's child, blue eyes and all. In the quietness of the moment, she knew she had to talk with Nathan about the upcoming days. She knew this might be one of her last chances to spend some quality alone time with her baby boy, but she struggled with how to begin.

"Honey, would you mind making me something warm to drink?" she asked Jack, her eyes imploring him to leave the room.

Jack jumped from his seat, knowing what his wife was about to say. They had talked about it the previous days, how and what and when to tell Nathan. Maggie's condition was rapidly worsening. Neither Jack nor Maggie talked about time, but they both knew it was running out.

"Sure," he said, exiting to the kitchen.

"Mrs. Patterson always thinks up such fun things for you to do," Maggie said to Nathan. "What was the story you had to write a few weeks ago that I liked so much?"

"About the frogs?"

"No. I liked that one a lot, but wasn't there one about flowers?"

"Oh yeah!" his eyes beamed. "What are flowers thinking underneath all the snow."

Maggie smiled at her son's enthusiasm. He had always loved helping her in the flower beds. When he was just a toddler, she would point to the smallest dot of green in the ground and say "Look, Nathan, here it comes," and then day by day they'd watch the flowers grow and bloom throughout the spring and summer.

Maggie repositioned herself, fighting back tears as she spoke to her son.

"You know, a lot of things are going to be happening over the next few weeks," she began slowly. "And a lot of it might be confusing to you."

Nathan was already confused, and his look told her so.

"Nathan," she soothed. "One day when you're older you might want to blame God for making me sick, but I don't want you to do that." Nathan frowned, bewildered. Why was his mother talking about being sick? He had always assumed that she would get better because really sick people were the ones who were in the hospital. "I want you to always know that God didn't make me sick, He helped me through this sickness," she comforted. "He gave me strength to play with you and Rachel and held me on my really horrible days."

Nathan put his head down. He didn't like talking about his mother's sickness. Maggie struggled to find the right words to say to her eight-year-old son.

"In a little while," she said slowly, "you may hear grown-ups say things like, 'Isn't it a pity? God took her so young.' But they're wrong, Nathan. They're wrong, and I don't want you to listen to them. When they say things like that, I want you to remember what I'm telling you now. God didn't take me, He received me."

Nathan's forehead crinkled as he looked at his mother. Maggie looked into her son's frightened eyes. Maybe what she was telling him was too much for him to understand.

"You mean in heaven, Mama?" he asked in nearly a whisper.

It broke Maggie's heart to hear him say it.

"Yes, sweetie, in heaven."

Nathan paused. Jack listened from the kitchen.

"God's going to take you to heaven?" Nathan asked, confused.

"No," Maggie assured. "He's not going to take me, Nathan. He's going to open His arms and receive me. There's a big difference, and I always want you to remember that."

Nathan fidgeted with the story in his hands and quietly asked, "What will you do there?"

"I can't even imagine," Maggie said, her voice faltering. "I know for the longest time I'll just be looking at God and thanking Him over and over for sending Jesus at Christmas and for the life He gave me here with you. It's going to be so beautiful there Nathan that I can't even begin to think what I'll be doing, but I know I won't be sick anymore." Nathan looked up at his mother. Maggie smiled. "I'll be completely healthy and I'll be running and jumping and playing and dancing just like I used to do with you before I got sick."

Nathan studied the paper in his hands for a long time. He didn't like talking to his mother about this. He didn't like how it made him feel.

"Will there be animals there?" he finally asked curiously.

"The most beautiful animals I've ever seen," Maggie answered, to the amazement of her son. "The animals that God created here for us on earth aren't anything compared to the animals in heaven. The zebra and giraffe? They'll look like common house cats compared to the animals in heaven."

"And none of them will be mean, right?" Nathan inquired anxiously.

"No. None of them will be mean. They'll be gentle and beautiful, and you can ride them and play with them all day long."

"Will the streets really be gold?"

Maggie smiled.

"The streets will be gold, and there will be beautiful rivers and waterfalls and the most beautiful land-scaping I've ever seen."

"The flowers will be prettier than yours?" he asked, surprised.

"Much prettier than mine," Maggie laughed. "The

94

flowers and trees will be much more beautiful than anything God ever created on earth." She stopped and allowed Nathan to process what she was saying.

"Will you see Grandpa there?" he finally asked, staring at his swinging legs.

"Yes," she smiled. "He'll be at the gate waiting for me." Her eyes filled with tears, and she turned her head away.

Nathan thought for a few moments, stopped swinging his legs, and then asked faintly, staring at his feet, "Why do you have to go?"

In the kitchen, Jack buried his head in his arms.

"Because Mommy's sick, and I just can't get better," Maggie answered softly.

"Will I be able to go with you?" he asked, his voice frightened at what his mother was telling him. Maggie clenched the bed sheet and twisted it, tears rimming her eyes.

"No, sweetie, you can't go with Mommy."

Tears ran down Nathan's face as he sprang to his mother's side, holding onto her. "I don't want you to go there without me," he sobbed. She wrapped her arms around his small back. In a short time she wouldn't have the strength to do that anymore. She hugged him tighter to her.

"I don't want to go without you either," she said, tears streaming down her face. "I'd give anything in the world to stay here with you, but I can't. I have to go."

"No, Mama—no!" the little boy implored, his tiny

fingers digging into his mother. "I don't want you to leave me."

Maggie wiped her face and pulled Nathan from her, wiping his tears away.

"Just because I'm leaving doesn't mean I'm not always going to be with you," she soothed. Maggie knew Nathan clearly didn't understand what she was saying, as his bottom lip began to quiver. She cupped his face gently in her hands. "I may not be around but I'm always going to be alive right in here," she said touching his chest. "That's where my dad lived after he went to heaven and that's where I'll always live in you, right inside your heart." He laid his head on his mother's chest, and she softly scratched his back.

"I want you to always know," she said, whispering to him, "that the greatest joy in my life is being your mommy." She turned his face toward hers and kissed his forehead. Looking into his eyes, she prayed that he would remember this night. That one day it would give him peace—that it would give him hope at Christmas.

She hugged him tightly, kissing every part of his face as the boy squirmed and started giggling in her arms. "You'd better get ready for bed, Little Man."

Jack stood in the kitchen, wiping his eyes with a dishtowel before heading into the living room. He didn't want his son to see him crying, then thought twice about that. Maybe it would be good to let Nathan see him crying, to show him that it was allowed, that everyone did.

"Go on back to your room, Nathan," Jack said, "and I'll be back to tuck you in in a minute."

"Love you," Maggie said, kissing the little boy again.

"I love you too, Mama," he replied, kissing her good night.

Nathan made his way down the hall, unaware of how the conversation would one day affect him. A flood of emotion washed over Maggie's face. Jack sweetly kissed her eyes and wiped her tears. He would try to explain it all to Nathan, someday when he was older. He would explain it again and again until Nathan understood.

SIX

Every happening, great or small, is a parable
whereby God speaks to us, and the art of life is to
get the message.
—Malcolm Muggeridge

Gwen!" I shouted out my door. "Did you reschedule the Alberto Diaz conference?" I waited for her to answer before impatiently getting up from my desk to look for her. When I saw her empty chair, I remembered that I'd let her leave three hours ago. It was Christmas Eve, and she had relatives to pick up at the airport. I sighed, looking at my watch.

"Seven o'clock," I said aloud to the empty office. I looked at my desk and groaned at the stack of files that had been sitting there since morning. I shoved a couple of the more important ones into my briefcase. I'd meant to knock off at five because I still hadn't done any Christmas shopping. Sometimes when I worked, I was in the habit of concentrating so hard that I occasionally failed to notice the passage of time.

After flipping off the office lights, I locked the door and rushed down the hall for the elevators. Aggravated, I pushed the button and wrestled with my coat as I stepped inside the doors. I rode to the ground floor alone, stewing in my thoughts. "This is just great," I grumbled. "Where can I find a store open so late on Christmas Eve?"

Just two days earlier I had driven to my mother's after work. Since Kate had asked me to leave, my life felt as if it was spinning out of control, and I had no idea of how to get it back on track. Mom was always a good sounding board. I pulled up in front of her house, but all the lights were off inside. Of course they were. It was 10:45. How could I ever expect to get my life back on track when I couldn't even leave the office at a decent hour? I sat in my car and marveled at my mother's house, twinkling with white lights, the Nativity shining brilliantly. She and my father had made our home a magical place to live. Birthdays were magical. Thanksgiving and Easter and Christmas were all magical. I used to joke with Kate that I believed in the Tooth Fairy till I was twenty-one because I never caught my mother sliding a quarter under my pillow. Mom and Dad wanted our home to be the most exciting place on earth for Hugh and me. Not a place of bickering, bitterness, and strife. They wanted to create magical memories, and they did. I leaned on the steering wheel and stared at the house. What magical memories would my girls remember of me? I shook my head and drove home, wondering how I could ever get the magic back.

Now I jumped into the Mercedes and wound my way through the brightly lit streets, heading downtown. Store windows sparkled with brilliant lights and decorations, but they were all closed. It was, no surprise, snowing again—large fat flakes filled the air. The streets were nearly empty, and I felt like the only person in the world who wasn't already home with his family. Even the tinkling of bells had stopped, as the Salvation Army ringers had already turned in their bright red pots for the night.

As I'd hoped, Wilson's department store was open. I'd tried to make a list at lunch, but I didn't know what anybody wanted.

I rushed, shouldering my way past other last-minute shoppers, to the toy department, where I found a large selection of Barbie dolls. Was Lily too young for Barbies? Was Hannah too old? How could you go wrong with a Barbie doll? I threw one in the shopping cart, trusting that Kate would be able to tell me which one of my daughters would like it more. In the electronics department, I picked up a Walkman for Hannah, who,

I figured, had to be about the right age to be discovering music, though who knew what kind of music she might like? In women's apparel I found a red cashmere sweater for my mother, then remembered that she already had a red sweater. I moaned and threw the sweater back on the pile without folding it, then picked it up again, thinking Kate might like it. A year ago I'd bought her a diamond necklace that cost me nearly five thousand dollars, because she'd been complaining that I didn't make her feel important, and I wanted to show her how much I cared. It hadn't changed a thing between us. I wasn't going to make the same mistake this year. I threw the sweater back down. I heard so many voices in my head. One said, "How could she?" One said, "What took her so long?" Another said, "If it's over, put it behind you as quickly as you can and move on—don't sit around moping." Yet another said, "But you love her, and she loves you—why isn't that enough?" Maybe separating would do us good, give us space to see clearly again. Maybe, I thought, she'd even miss me and come to her senses.

As I made my way through the store, I observed a little boy running through the aisles, touching every item on racks and shelves, much to the chagrin of the nearby store clerks. He ran straight into me as I was holding up a knit scarf for my mother. "Sorry, sir," he said breathlessly without looking up. I shook my head. I despised parents who let their children run unsupervised through stores. The little boy continued sifting through racks of clothing, moving around the circular stands, pulling out blouses, shirts, and jackets. I watched him. A rack toppled forward as he brushed it from behind. I looked around again for the kid's parents.

"Please watch what you're doing," I scolded the child, irritated.

Feeling aggravated and exhausted, I had thrown a few more items into the basket when I passed the little boy again, now nervously bounding into the women's-shoes department. I watched as the anxious boy touched or picked up nearly every boot, pump, and loafer in the department. Then a pair of shoes seemed to catch his eye on an overcrowded sales rack. He picked up the pair and, for a moment, he was still. The shoes were shiny silver, aglow with red, blue, and green rhinestones and shimmering sequins. The boy tucked them under his arm and hurried in the direction of the register. "Just my luck," I thought as I made my way to the checkout line, my shopping done, taking my place behind him. The boy fidgeted, shifting his weight from one foot to the other, as the cashier took forever to ring out the customers ahead of us. Again, I glanced sideways to see if the child's parents were nearby.

As the boy swung the glittery shoes, I finally had to smile. The child obviously didn't want his mother to see him buy the shoes for her. He began to pace.

I looked down at the items in my basket and wondered when was the last time I had anxiously raced around a department store looking for the perfect gift for someone.

When my brother and I were young, our arms would ache from shaking every last cent out of our piggy banks. We'd stuff our pockets until they bulged with the heavy coins and walk excitedly to the local five-and-dime. Rummaging through trays of pins, we would earnestly look for the one with the biggest fake diamonds for our mother, and then we'd run to the men's aisle for the adventure of finding the ideal Christmas tie for our father. One year we skipped getting him a tie and got him a three-foot-long shoehorn instead, one he wouldn't have to bend over to use. It used to be so exciting, Hugh and myself scurrying, stumbling, and fumbling through the store, nearly bursting from the thought of Mom and Dad opening their presents on Christmas Day.

The little boy moved forward and placed the shoes down for the cashier to scan the price—$14.25. The child dug into the pockets of his worn jeans and pulled out a small crumpled wad of bills and scattered change. The cashier straightened out the mess of currency.

"There's only $4.60 here, son," he said.

"How much are the shoes?" the child inquired, concerned.

"They're $14.25," the cashier replied. "You'll need to get some more money from your mom or dad."

Visibly upset, the boy asked, "Can I bring the rest of the money tomorrow?"

The cashier smiled and shook his head no, scooping up the change.

Tears pooled in the child's eyes.

He turned around and said, "Sir, I need to buy those shoes for my mother," his voice shaking. I was startled to see that the child was talking to me. I felt the hairs stand up on the back of my neck. "She's not been feeling very good, and when we were eating dinner my dad said that Mama might leave to see Jesus tonight."

I stood unmoving, holding the basket.

I didn't know what to say.

"I want her to look beautiful when she meets Jesus," he said, his eyes beseeching me.

Why is he asking me? I thought. Do I look like an easy target—the rich man with money to throw around? I instantly felt annoyed. Was this some sort of con, parents sending their children out to take advantage of people's emotions at Christmas? Yet, why did the child tell the cashier he'd bring the rest of the money tomorrow?

I didn't know what to say or how to react. All I knew was it was suddenly more than I could take. This kid was no scam artist, somehow I knew that. I looked into his wide eyes and something happened to me in that moment. A pair of shoes to meet Jesus in. This child is losing his mother.

Without thinking or saying a word, I pulled out my wallet and handed the cashier a fifty-dollar bill to pay the remainder of the cost of the shoes.

The little boy lifted onto his tiptoes and watched as the last of the money was distributed into the drawer. Eagerly, he grabbed the package, then turned and stopped for a moment, looking at me again.

"Thank you," was all he said.

I watched as the child ran out the door and disappeared into the streets.

"Are you ready, sir?" the cashier asked. I didn't hear what he was saying. "Sir?" he asked again. "Are you ready to cash out?"

I looked at the items in my basket and shook my head.

"No," I answered. "I think I need to start over."

I left the full basket on the cashier's counter and slowly walked out the front doors. I put the Mercedes into gear and drove through the streets of town to Adams Hill, where, through the heavily falling snow, I could see Kate's bedroom light on upstairs.

The whole drive home I didn't know what I would say or how to say it. I just knew that I had to get there. I had to get the magic back. Suddenly, my life depended on it. Kate was right. My family wasn't leaving me, I'd left them. When did that happen? How did I get so lost? Home. The word all at once felt new. What had once been a place of emptiness was now one of joy, a place of refuge from life's unpredictable sorrow. A place of hope. I was going home at last.

I couldn't help it. I knew it was late, but the minute I entered the door I shouted, "Kate! Kate!"

Kate ran down the stairs, heatedly shushing me not

to wake the girls, who were already in bed. Without saying a word, I guided Kate onto the sofa and knelt in front of her.

"What is wrong with you?" she asked.

"Listen to me," I began slowly. "I didn't get you or the girls anything for Christmas."

"I didn't expect you to get me anything," she answered hotly, throwing my hands from her shoulders. "But I thought you'd at least want to get your own children something." She attempted to push herself off the sofa and away from me, but I pressed her firmly back into the cushions.

"What are you doing, Robert?" she demanded, her cheeks flushed.

"Kate, I'm begging you. I don't really know what to say, but I need you to listen to me." She yanked her arms from me, crossing them in front of her.

"What?" she snapped.

I gathered my thoughts and began slowly.

"I didn't buy anything because I didn't know what to buy." She set her chin and stared at me, but she was listening, and that's all I wanted. "I didn't know what to buy because I don't know any of you," I continued. "I have let all of you slip away from me, to the point of where you're actually strangers now." Kate sat unmoved by my words or emotions.

"What?" she asked, bewildered.

I rose and sat square in front of her on the coffee table.

"Kate," I pleaded. "I went to the store. I went there

to buy things for you and Mom and the girls. I was even in line to cash out when it hit me. . . ." I wasn't sure how to put any of my feelings into words. Kate arched her eyebrows for me to continue. "You all are the greatest gifts in the world," I said, selecting my words carefully, "but I don't treat you like a gift. I don't treat the girls like gifts."

She shifted uncomfortably, not sure how she should react to what I was saying.

"The greatest possible gift I could give to you or the girls would be myself," I went on. "I need to give you the respect and love you deserve, and I need to give the girls time and attention and piggyback rides and trips to the zoo and amusement parks and I don't know what else," I said, clasping my head in my hands. "I need to give them a dad. They've had a provider," I continued. "They've had some guy in the house who they've told people was their father, but they've never had a dad. I want to be with them, not just in the same room with them. I want to be with them and share in everything that makes them happy. I want to be there when they fail. I want us to be there," I said, looking at her. I peered into Kate's eyes, looking for the smallest glint of hope or acceptance. She was understandably skeptical—we'd logged a lot of years of hurt and anger together.

"Kate," I said, then stopped. "I don't know how you feel." I leaned on my knees and rubbed my hands together, thinking. "I don't know if you're really ready for us to end because . . . because I don't think I am."

"Why the sudden change of heart?" she asked, her tone still doubtful.

"I don't know, Kate," I replied, shaking my head. "All I know is it's Christmas." She looked at me, confused. "It's Christmas, Kate, and I realized that nobody could give me a greater gift than that of my family."

She shook her head and looked away. I gently took hold of her arms and turned her toward me. She looked anxiously into my eyes.

"Nothing matters to me, Kate," I said, slightly squeezing her arms in my grip. "Nothing. The job, the cars, the house. None of it. The only thing that matters to me is you and Hannah and Lily because . . ." I stopped, concerned that she would never believe me, but I knew I had to say it. "Because I love all of you." I stopped to watch her face. Her expression was one of puzzled wonderment. It was the same look she used to give me when we were dating, when I'd say something that she thought was crazy. It was the exact same look, and I was warmed by the fact that I recognized it.

"I do, Kate," I whispered. "I love you and I don't want to lose you."

Kate searched my eyes. What was in them tonight? Hope? Forgiveness? Peace? I released my hold and she fell back into the sofa, still watching me. I wasn't burying myself in the mail or running away from her to go to the office but, instead, I felt filled to the very brim with some sort of joy. Joy. I wasn't anxious or restless or upset about anything. I was truly calm and serene, in an inexplicably strange, peaceful way. I hadn't been calm and serene in years.

She crossed her legs and asked slowly, "What happened to you tonight?"

"It's a long story," I said, smiling, and then we talked into the night.

Maggie's breathing was labored, but she was coherent. Sylvia prepared to switch the IV bag, but Maggie lifted her hand weakly to stop her. Sylvia had hooked up a new bag that morning, yet throughout the day it had slowly drained empty, and she needed to replace it with a full bag that would take Maggie through the evening.

"Maggie," Sylvia whispered, "this will help with your pain."

"No," Maggie mouthed.

"It's okay, Sylvia," Jack said. "She wants to watch the kids unwrap their presents. She knows she won't be able to if you give her that."

Sylvia stroked Maggie's cheek and straightened the scarf on her head.

"All right, baby doll," she comforted. "I'm going to leave this right here," she added, hooking the bag on the pole beside Maggie's bed. "If you want some medicine, just have somebody open up the drip, all right?" Maggie nodded and Sylvia smiled, squeezing her arm. "You just yell if you need me," she said to Jack, slipping to Rachel's room, where she would work on a needlepoint stocking or read when she wanted to give Jack and Maggie as much uninterrupted time as she could. She had been with them ten to twelve hours a day for the last two weeks, going home some time in the evening. Sylvia held the needlework in her hands and rested her head against the wall. She would be finishing up her shift in another thirty minutes, leaving the Andrews family to spend Christmas Eve alone.

Normally, Jack and Maggie would retrieve presents from the attic once Nathan had gone to bed, but this year Jack suggested they unwrap their gifts on Christmas Eve instead of waiting for Christmas morning. He and Evelyn had wrapped what few presents they had for the children and placed them under the tree days ago.

Evelyn went into the bathroom and brought out some blush, eye shadow, powder, and lipstick to Maggie's bedside. When Maggie was no longer strong enough to put on her own makeup, Evelyn did it for her. Evelyn gently freshened the colors she had applied that morning—a soft taupe to Maggie's eyelids, dusty mauve to her sunken cheeks, and rosewood to her lips. She finished by dusting Maggie's face with some fresh powder, then held up a mirror for Maggie to see herself.

"Thanks, Mom," she whispered feebly.

Nathan tiptoed in through the backdoor and into his room, unnoticed. After dinner he had told his father he needed to run to a neighbor's house down the street. Jack assumed Nathan and his little friend had made gifts for everyone and didn't question him any further. After a few minutes, Nathan carefully opened his bedroom door and tiptoed down the hall and into the living room, depositing the gift under the tree.

Jack had tried to get ready for this evening, hoping it would never come. As hard as he prayed, he just wasn't ready for this to be his last Christmas with Maggie. He sat by her bed earlier in the day and watched her sleep. How could she be so sick and still be so beautiful? How could he ever wake up in a house without her in it? He watched as she drew in small, shallow breaths. The look in Sylvia's eyes told him it wouldn't be long, that she'd started to let go. Two days ago Sylvia sat Jack down and talked to him about helping Maggie go—letting her know that it was okay, that she didn't have to hold on anymore.

Maggie woke to the same eyes she'd fallen in love with nearly twelve years earlier. "I love you," she whispered. There weren't enough hours in the day for them to say those words, but they said them as often as they could.

"I love you, Maggie," Jack answered softly. "I always have and I always will."

She smiled and moved her fingers toward him.

He stood up, holding the fragile hand in his and kissed her lightly.

"That broken down Ford Escort was the greatest thing that ever happened to me," he said slowly. Her eyes twinkled. How fortunate she was to have had someone who loved her so completely for so long.

They talked about her mother and the kids and about taking care of her flowers in the spring. Jack talked about everything he could think of, rambling and groping for words as Maggie nodded and smiled. He caressed her face and held her hand, repeatedly saying "I love you" until she fell back to sleep, listening to his voice.

For dinner, Evelyn warmed up some turkey someone from church had dropped off, complete with gravy and stuffing and cranberry sauce. After the dinner dishes were set aside, Jack started pulling the few presents from under the tree and handed one to Nathan to unwrap. Rachel sat on Evelyn's lap, squirming and clapping her hands.

"Hurry up and hand this child a present before she bursts," Evelyn laughed. Maggie smiled as Rachel tightly squeezed the stuffed Pooh bear with the big, fat, soft tummy. Nathan's eyes lit up when he saw the new Matchbox cars he'd been wanting.

"I'm taking these to show-and-tell," he cried.

Jack winked at Maggie and held her hand as Rachel screamed, "Oh my! Oh my!" when she unwrapped a pink baby doll whose eyes actually moved. Nathan beamed with excitement at the package of ten different colored markers he held in his hands.

Evelyn unwrapped a beautiful purple and black scarf to go with her winter coat that Nathan and Rachel picked out themselves.

"It's so warm and toasty," she said, kissing her grandchildren.

Bending over, Evelyn pulled out a skinny box and handed it to Jack.

"We weren't supposed to exchange gifts," he said, feeling terribly sorry that there wasn't one under the tree for her.

"I know," Evelyn replied. "It's just something I thought you might like," she said, smiling at Maggie.

He opened it and pulled out a framed crayon drawing of a little girl with big circles of red on her cheeks and hair that flipped up at the ends. She was wearing a blue dress with big yellow flowers on it and holding a red balloon. Her arms were long and straight and both feet turned in the same direction, one clearly bigger than the other. Beside her stood a puffy white dog with a smile on its face, its four legs long and spider-like, all of them facing the same direction. By the dog's paws in big, red letters, the drawing was signed *Maggie*. Jack smiled broadly and thanked Evelyn, holding up the artwork for Maggie to see.

"She was in kindergarten when she drew that," Evelyn explained. "I found it in my things a while ago and told Maggie I'd get it framed for you."

Jack held the picture and imagined Maggie drawing it, wishing he could have seen her as a little girl rummaging through her crayons strewn all around her and carefully selecting the perfect one to color in the flowers or the right shade of blue for the dress. He clutched the drawing and leaned over to kiss Maggie.

"I'll hang it right next to the da Vinci," he said, holding her hand.

Nathan anxiously waited for his mother to open his present, the anticipation giving him butterflies. He scurried under the tree and pulled out a small box. There were only two more presents under the tree— he'd counted. Jack stood by Maggie and gently tore into the wrapping paper for her. It was a small jewelry box. Jack lifted the lid. In the center of the blue velvet padding was a delicate gold locket with a rose etched into the front of it. Jack opened the locket to reveal a picture of Rachel laughing at the camera in her red Christmas dress on one side and Nathan sitting on the front porch when all the flowers were in bloom on the other side.

"Oh," Maggie said, smiling.

"I know you've always wanted one of these with pictures of the kids," Jack said, putting it around her neck.

"This," Evelyn explained holding a present in her hand, "is something else she has always wanted."

Maggie looked at her mother quizzically as Evelyn softly tore the tissue wrapping paper around the gift. Evelyn lifted the lid to reveal her crimson satin wrap, the one Maggie had always adored. Evelyn had received it as a present from her own mother and had worn it draped over her shoulders in her wedding picture. She was wearing a skirt, a soft blouse, a corsage, a hat, and the beautiful wrap. Maggie's eyes lit up.

"She has always had her eye on this," Evelyn teased, draping it around Maggie's shoulders. "Thank you," Maggie mouthed. Evelyn kissed her forehead and fussed with the wrap till it was tied elegantly in front.

Nathan crawled under the tree again. It was finally time for his present. Reaching toward the back, he pulled out the haphazardly wrapped package he'd shoved under the tree just minutes earlier. He placed the package on his mother's lap, and Evelyn and Jack exchanged glances as Nathan helped his mother tear the wrapping. Together they ripped into the plain brown paper. Nathan eagerly helped his mother lift the lid off the box. Nathan reached in and pulled out the sparkly shoes for his mother. Her eyes gleamed as she held the shoes on her chest, admiring them. Nathan hurried excitedly to the foot of the bed, uncovering Maggie's legs, triumphantly slipping the shoes onto his mother's feet.

"They're the prettiest shoes they had," he told her.

"They're so beautiful," she whispered, smiling at her proud son.

We arrived at my mother's house early Christmas Day. "Merry Christmas!" Mom yelled as she flung open the door. The air was filled with aromas of roast turkey, mulled cider, pecan pie, evergreen, and aged oak logs burning in the fireplace. Hannah and Lily ran screaming into their grandmother's arms, falling over each other to get to their presents under the tree.

"Merry Christmas, Mom!" Kate laughed as Hannah frantically dragged her to the tree.

"Merry Christmas, Mom," I said leaning in to kiss

her. I was eager to tell her about what had happened last night.

"Come on!" Lily shouted as she threw herself against my legs.

"Okay, okay," I relented. "Let's get things started here."

Lily banged her tiny hands together as I handed her a present that she swore was bigger than anything she'd ever seen. Hannah gasped when a beautiful gold box with gold lace ribbon was given to her. I passed out the gifts until everyone had their very own pile in front of them—sweaters, earrings, cookware, and books for Kate; baby dolls, coloring books, clothes, and more baby dolls for Lily; then a beautiful grown-up necklace for Hannah, along with games, elegant paper dolls and the latest Barbie accessories. Kate had shopped weeks earlier for Mom. She unwrapped a gorgeous brooch with the birthstones of all her grand-children embedded in a circle of gold.

"I have always wanted one of these!" she shouted. "I'm going to wear it everywhere," she exclaimed, proudly pinning it to her sweater. The new pin would also fit nicely on the lapel of her brand-new peri-winkle blazer and red silk blouse. "Oh, how beau-tiful," she cried, squeezing Lily's cheeks. "What a fashionable granny I'll be."

I set aside my new aftershave, books, socks, and underwear. Why, after so many years, did my mother insist on buying me underwear?

"I assumed you were running low on boxers," she

teased, to the infectious giggles of her granddaughters.

"I was, Mother. Thank you," I said, grinning, ripping into the last present from my pile. I tore back the paper and ran my thumbnail across the tape holding the small box shut. Lifting the lid, I carefully opened the edges of the tissue paper and looked at Mother in surprise. I pulled out the Dunhill Billiard and held it up, reading the card she had slipped into the box. "No regrets," it stated simply.

"What's that?" Kate asked, surprised.

"This," I said, pushing the end of the pipe proudly into my mouth with the flare of a British statesman, "is a reminder."

Mom was bent over, opening the oven door, when I snuck up on her.

"Mom," I said anxiously.

Startled, she snapped upright, slamming the door with a bang. "Don't scare me, Robert," she scolded.

"I didn't mean to," I said, ushering her to the kitchen table.

"I didn't check on my turkey," she claimed, spinning on her heels.

"Wait," I urged. "Sit down." She sat. "Mom, last night Kate and I talked till four-thirty in the morning."

"About what?" she exclaimed. "My word, you must be exhausted."

"I am," I said, rubbing my temples. "I'm dog tired. I could throw up, I'm so tired."

"Well, don't stand over me!" she shouted, laughing.

I sat down, my eyes flashing.

"Mom, the most incredible thing happened last night." She sat forward, listening. "It was like an epiphany, like a lightning bolt hit me or something. I was shopping for all of you when I decided not to get anybody anything. Oh, by the way—Kate bought you the brooch and stuff," I offered as an aside. "I didn't know anything about it."

"Thanks a lot," she roared.

"Really long story short—we're going to try to work it out."

She banged on the table. "I knew she still loved you."

"I think she does," I said shyly. "And I know I love her."

"Well, go," she commanded, shooing me toward the door. "Go, go, go! Go play with your girls on Christmas. I'll keep things going in here and will be out in a minute." She playfully shoved me out the door and moved to the oven.

"Thank you, Lord!" I could hear her whoop from the living room. I heard the oven door creak open and then the metallic swish of a carving knife being sharpened against steel. "Thank you," echoed from the kitchen, amid the clamoring of pots and pans. "Thank you! Thank you! Thank you!"

SEVEN

We are not necessarily doubting that God will do the best for us; we are wondering how painful the best will turn out to be.
—C. S. Lewis

It was nearing midnight. The lights on the tree blazed faithfully. The children were sound asleep. Nathan was probably too old to dream of Santa Claus, and Rachel was too young. Jack looked into his wife's blue eyes for as long as she could hold them open.

"I love you, Maggie," he said over and over. "Thank you for being my wife. Thank you for loving me." She was unable to speak but held Jack's gaze. "We're going to be okay, Maggie," he said, holding her face. "We all love you, and we're going to be okay, so it's all right if you want to go now."

Evelyn stroked Maggie's arms and held her hand.

"You don't have to hold on anymore," Jack comforted.

"Your daddy's waiting for you," Evelyn added. "You can go be with your daddy, and we'll all be okay here."

Maggie's eyes eventually closed, and for the next two hours, Evelyn and Jack continued to talk to her, watching as each breath became shallower, a low rattle building in her chest. Evelyn read the Christmas story from Luke. "So Joseph also went up from the town of Nazareth in Galilee to Judea, to Bethlehem the town of David," she read. Jack straightened the wrap around Maggie's shoulders and positioned the locket in the center of her chest. "He went there to register with Mary," Evelyn continued, "who was pledged to be married to him and was expecting a child. While they were there, the time came for the baby to be born, and she gave birth to her firstborn, a son." Evelyn paused, stroking Maggie's hand as she read on. "She wrapped him in cloths and placed him in a manger, because there was no room for them in the inn." Evelyn continued to read about the shepherds in their fields and realized the Book of Luke didn't include the Wise Men. Flipping back to the Book of Matthew, she quickly found the passage she was looking for.

"Here it is, Maggie," she said holding the Bible up toward her daughter. "After Jesus was born in Bethlehem in Judea, during the time of King Herod, Magi from the east came to Jerusalem and asked, 'Where is the one who has been born king of the Jews? We saw his star in the east and have come to worship him.'" Evelyn laid the Bible on her lap. "When she was little, Maggie would always say that she couldn't believe no one else even bothered to notice that huge star in the sky. Remember that, Maggie?" Evelyn asked, caressing her face. "Look for that star now, Maggie.

We're all okay here. Nathan and Rachel are warm and asleep in their beds. We're all going to be okay, so look for the star and follow it. Follow it till you find Jesus. He's waiting for you, baby."

Jack and Evelyn recalled sweet memories for another hour. They talked about Maggie on her wedding day, and of Nathan's and Rachel's births. Jack told Maggie over and over again how beautiful she was, and how she had completed his life, and at 2:43 A.M., as he uttered once more how much he loved her, she took one final breath and died. There was no more pain. No more suffering. No more labored breaths.

Evelyn stood motionless beside the bed, her hand trembling over her mouth.

"Oh God, no," she moaned, burying her head into Maggie's shoulder. "I'm not ready for her to go." Jack crumpled beside the bed, still holding Maggie's hand, his heaving shoulders shaking the bed with each broken sob.

"Oh, my sweet angel," Evelyn wailed, kissing Maggie's face and hands. "My sweet, sweet angel."

Jack pulled Maggie into his arms and rocked her back and forth, the bright colored scarf slipping from her head. "I thought I was ready to let you go, Maggie, but I'm not," he sobbed into her neck. "I'm just not."

It was shortly after 3 A.M. when Jack awakened Nathan and explained that Mommy had stepped into heaven. Nathan ran, frightened, into the living room, where he saw his mother lying peacefully. His grandmother was holding and stroking his mother's hand. Evelyn's face was red and wet with tears. Nathan stood by his mother's bed and tenderly touched her hand. It didn't reach out for him, or draw him close to her, but lay motionless on the bed. Nathan felt his father's hand on his shoulder as he looked into his mother's face. She looked as if she was sleeping.

"Is she already in heaven?" he asked softly, closely watching for his mother's chest to rise and fall in breath.

"She is, darlin'," his grandmother said, smiling, tears falling from her chin. "She's already there."

Before the men from the funeral-home arrived, they each said good-bye, kissing Maggie's face and her hands, stroking her arms, and caressing her cheek. "I love you, Mama," Nathan sobbed, falling into his father. It was more than his eight-year-old mind could comprehend, that he would never see his mother again.

There would be those in town who would say it was cruel for Jack to wake Nathan the night his mother died, but one day Nathan would be thankful for the time he had had with his father and grandmother as they each, in their own special way, said good-bye to her. He saw the peace on his mother's face and knew that what she had told him was true. That even at that very moment she was in heaven.

Although they were expecting it, the soft knock on the door startled them all. Jack moved to the entryway, feeling as if he were moving in slow motion. He opened the door. Two men spoke softly to Jack as he motioned them in. Evelyn pulled Nathan to her as they watched the men work in silence, gently placing Maggie's sheeted body on a collapsible stretcher. Jack kept a hand on his wife as the men wheeled her out into the cold and into the back of the hearse. Nathan stood beside the empty bed as his grandmother fell broken into the chair beside it, pulling him down on her lap, wrapping her arms tightly around him, sobbing. Beyond the window, snow gracefully fell to earth. Nathan's father stayed outside in the cold and watched the hearse back out onto the street and drive away.

The phone rang at eleven o'clock on Christmas morning. Doris had been busily chatting away with her son and daughter-in-law, everyone making their way through the great pile of gifts on the floor under the tree. Doris hurried into the kitchen and picked up the receiver. Her face fell as she listened to the voice on the other end of the line. She didn't know the person calling, an aunt, she thought she heard her say, or maybe it was a neighbor—she couldn't recall. The only thing she heard was that Maggie Andrews had died peacefully at home last night. Jack and her mother were by her side.

By one o'clock that afternoon, Nathan's home swelled with friends, relatives, and neighbors, and the countertops overflowed with food—turkey, gravy, dressing, green beans, peas, corn, and every potato imaginable: mashed potatoes, scalloped potatoes, cheesy potatoes, sweet potatoes, sweet potato casserole.

Nathan pulled a Santa cookie from a Tupperware container his grandmother kept them in and sat quietly on the floor in the corner. His father and grandmother emerged from the bedroom carrying everything his mother would be buried in, the favorite dress she often wore to church and weddings, along with the beautiful wrap his grandmother had given her, and the sparkly shoes Nathan had purchased. He observed quietly as the grown-ups consoled his father and grandmother, clasping Jack on the back or squeezing his arm and whispering in his ear. He recognized the men his father worked with in the crowd, and the people from church. Rachel toddled through the forest of long legs, swinging Pooh bear in her hand as she crawled onto her father's lap. A small group of women shook their heads somberly and patted his grandmother's arm.

Nathan recognized some neighbors. He wasn't sure who a lot of the adults were, maybe people from Ferguson's, where his mother used to work. Many of them slipped quietly in, leaving food or gifts on the kitchen table and then slipped back out without saying a word. The faces would blur, but Nathan would always remember their quiet acts of generosity. One elderly woman wearing a Christmas Is Love sweatshirt washed every dish, scrubbed every pan, emptied the garbage, and straightened and tidied the kitchen unnoticed. Drying her hands, she moved stealthily to the living room, where, when Nathan craned his neck, he could see her gathering cups, saucers, and plates, and taking them to the kitchen, where she promptly washed them, dried them, and put them away. She tackled the refrigerator next, dumping moldy dishes, wiping down shelves and making room for the many casserole and Corning Ware dishes of food that were sitting on the countertops and the table. When the food was in order and her work was done, she slid on her coat and left.

Another couple appeared in the front door, said a few words to Jack and Evelyn, and quietly bundled Rachel up, gathering Pooh, her new pink baby doll, and some clothes, and shuffled out the door as Jack planted a kiss on one of his daughter's plump, red cheeks. Nathan was glad that no one was whisking him away. Although his mother was not here, he knew, even then, that these moments were part of her and something he needed to share in.

He looked toward the front door when he heard the familiar voice of his teacher, Mrs. Patterson, saying hello in the entryway. He hadn't expected to see her until after Christmas break. When he saw her gentle face, his throat tightened. They hadn't said much to each other all those days she'd driven him home from school, but he'd come to look forward to the time they'd spent together in the car. A kind-looking man Nathan had never seen before was with her. Nathan watched as the couple spoke with his father and grandmother, Mrs. Patterson's arm around his grandmother's shoulders. Nathan sprung to his feet and walked toward his teacher.

"Hello, Nathan," Doris said warmly. She looked to Nathan as though she may have been crying.

"Hi, Mrs. Patterson," he said quietly, waving the Santa cookie in his hand.

"Nathan, this is Mr. Patterson," she said, holding her husband's hand.

"Very nice to meet you, Nathan," the man with the gentle face said.

Nathan was glad that his teacher and her nice husband came to visit today.

Doris guided Nathan to the kitchen table and sat down. He carefully placed his Santa cookie on the table in front of him.

"Nathan," Doris began. "I forgot all about the roll of film this picture was on. I found it when I was tidying my desk drawers for Christmas break. I thought you might like to have this." She pulled out a framed photo of Maggie and Nathan taken the first week of school, when they'd helped decorate the classroom bulletin board. Before the picture was snapped, Maggie held up two yellow pipe cleaners behind Nathan's head, laughing gleefully when the flash went off.

From an envelope, Doris pulled out two other pictures. In one, Maggie was sitting at a tiny table in the school hallway, holding up a flash card to a student intently studying it. As the school photographer had walked toward them, Maggie turned and grinned. In the second picture, she had leaned over the table, pressing her face, cheek to cheek, into the student's, as if they were crammed into a photo booth at the mall, her arm extended over her head, a broad smile running the width of her face.

"Those two were taken last year," Doris said, smiling.

Nathan stared at the photos, shuffling through the three of them like a deck of cards, the framed one to the top, then the top to the bottom, carefully examining and reexamining each one. His mom looked different in the pictures . . . and then he realized why. They had been taken before she got sick, when she was still the mom who could jump in the leaves with him and dance around the house to the music on the radio and come to help out at his school. That's how he would always remember her, just as she was in the pictures.

They sat together quietly for several minutes before Doris stood and turned to leave.

"Thank you, Mrs. Patterson," Nathan said softly, fumbling the pictures in his hands.

Doris turned to him, wishing she had something to say, but she didn't know what that was. She and her husband were saying good-bye to Jack and Evelyn when Doris noticed the shiny, beaded shoes lying among a small pile of clothing near the front door. She turned toward Nathan, who smiled shyly.

"I wanted her to feel special and beautiful," was all

he said. Doris's eyes were wet with tears.

"Oh, darling, she did. I'm certain she did." She let go of her husband's hand and bent down and hugged Nathan tightly to her before closing the door behind her.

Nathan walked to the storm door and watched his teacher as she and her husband got into their car. He heard hushed fragments of a conversation in the hallway. He couldn't hear exactly what was being said, but heard enough to know that his mother wouldn't want him to listen. So he tuned out the voices, gazed at his mother's laughing face in the photo, and squinted into the sky, looking for her in the clouds.

The sun was rising in the sky, shimmering along the snowbanks and shining down on trees bending under the weight of the snow, when the phone rang. I had already completed a rousing game of hide-and-seek with Hannah and Lily when Kate called me from downstairs.

"It's Dalton," she said, handing me the receiver.

Dalton and Heddy were standing on the front porch waiting for Kate and me as I maneuvered the Mercedes into the driveway. I threw open the car door and stumbled past them into the house. I spun around the living room, frantically searching for Mother, bursting through the kitchen door, only to find it empty. I ran back into the living room, where I was met by the wet, grave faces of Dalton, Heddy, and Kate.

"Don't tell me, Dalton," I begged, falling in stunned silence to the sofa, my voice breaking. "Don't tell me she's not here." Kate sat beside me, wrapping her arms around me, leaning her head on my shoulder.

"She'd invited us over for breakfast," Dalton said soberly. "When she didn't answer the door, we let ourselves in with our own key and found her in her chair by the tree. The ambulance got here right away but. . . ." He stopped. This was heartbreaking for Dalton. He loved my mother very much. He stepped toward me and handed me a letter. "This was in her hand." I stuffed the paper into my pocket.

Nathan stood at the front door, watching as the hospital bed was wheeled out of the living room and loaded into the back of a medical-supplies truck parked in the driveway. He'd felt nervous and scared as the men loaded it, his heart beating faster and faster as the truck door slammed shut with a clang. As the truck backed out of the drive, his body filled with emotion. He shut the door against the cold winter air, pressing his nose against its wood, and wept softly.

He took a deep breath. He thought about all of the times he'd sat in school wondering where his mother or father was at that exact moment. What kind of car was Dad working on? What was Mom doing? Was she playing with Rachel? Maybe she was in the kitchen baking cookies for when he got home from school. Perhaps she was wheeling Rachel around in a shopping cart, buying groceries at Ferguson's. He often pictured what his mother was doing throughout the day, but now he'd no longer wonder. He knew exactly where she was and what she was doing. She was running and jumping and playing, just like she used to do with him before she ever had to get into that hospital bed. And in some peaceful, inexplicable way, that vision wrapped him in hope as he stood by the window and cried.

The coroner's office called later that evening. My mother had died of a brain aneurysm. The voice on the line explained that my mother had gone very quickly and felt no pain. I'd called Hugh and made a number of other calls to relatives and friends before kissing Hannah and Lily goodnight, holding them tightly in my arms.

Kate and I sat together in the living room, lit only by the tiny white lights of the Christmas tree.

"I was thinking we should bury her in the periwinkle jacket," I said, staring into the lights. "And the new blouse and pin." My voice faltered as I cleared my throat and continued softly. "She would definitely want the pin, because it has the stones of all her grandchildren in it."

I laughed, wiping the tears from my face.

"She'd never let me hear the end of it if I didn't bury her with the pin that represented all her grandbabies."

Kate rested her head on the back of the sofa, wiping the tears with both hands from her face.

"I'm going to ask Dalton to say something at the

funeral," I said. "I can't imagine anyone else doing it."

"I can't either," Kate reassured.

I glanced at my watch.

"Hugh's flight is at ten. They'll all get in at five-thirty tomorrow morning. We can plan the rest of the service with the pastor when he gets here." I leaned forward on the sofa and buried my face in my hands, rubbing tired, bloodshot eyes with the heels of my palms.

Kate scooted over, grabbed my hand, and set it on her lap, holding onto it as she fell asleep. I gently draped a throw over Kate and sat quietly in the stillness, staring at the Christmas tree, the way my mother had always loved to do. I recalled the day Hannah and Lily had decorated the tree, small hands digging anxiously through the boxes of decorations, each child clamoring to find the next prettiest bulb to hang on its branches. The tree was more than just a decoration to Mom. It was a daily reminder of the time she'd spent with her children and grandchildren. I wiped another tear from my face.

"What a lousy time of year to lose your mother," I said, rubbing my temples.

When my head started to bob, and I felt myself nodding off in the early-morning hours, I stood to retrieve a blanket from the hall closet for myself. I straightened Kate's legs on the sofa and started to empty my pants pockets when I felt the letter Dalton had given me earlier in the day. Amid all of the commotion, I had forgotten all about it.

I turned the letter toward the lights of the tree and began to read.

"Dear Robert," it began. "I know the hard part is just beginning, but one day you'll understand that it is worth it. . . . <u>All</u> of it."

I wept as I read the rest of the unfinished letter.

EIGHT

Death's power is limited—
It cannot eradicate memories
Or slay love
It cannot destroy even a threadbare faith
Or permanently hobble the smallest hope in God
It cannot permeate the soul
And it cannot cripple the spirit
It merely separates us for a while
That is the only power death can claim
—No more

—Donna VanLiere

It was late when the phone rang. Kate and I both leaped for it at once. Kate got there first. I watched her face as the expression changed from tense concern to utter happiness.

"It's a boy!" she shrieked. *I'm a grandfather—we're grandparents,* I thought, my heart brimming. "She wants to speak with you," Kate said, handing me the receiver.

"Hello, sweetie," I said, "Congratulations. How's my little girl?"

"I'm fine, Daddy. I'm perfect," Hannah replied. Her voice sounded strong, full.

"Well, how's our grandson?" I could hardly contain my joy.

"He's gorgeous, Daddy, but he's got Uncle Hugh's feet," she exclaimed.

"Oh my, bunions already?" I joked.

"No, but he is pigeon-toed. . . . Somehow they're pretty adorable on him, though," she laughed.

"Well, does the little fellow have a name?" I asked. There was a brief pause on the other end of the line.

"His name is Evan Robert," she said softly. "After you, Daddy."

Evan Robert had arrived! He weighed six pounds eleven ounces and was twenty-one inches long. He's a beautiful pink baby with soft tufts of hair on each side of his head, causing him to look very much like a little old man with a terribly receding hairline. Hannah and her husband, Steven, live four hours away in a small town where she teaches the fifth grade and he works as a state trooper. Hannah is most definitely her mother's daughter, from her shiny black hair to her melodious laugh and compassionate heart. It makes me smile to see the mirror image of the Kate I first met so many years ago. Lily is finishing her last year of college and since interning at my firm this past summer, has been threatening to pursue a career in law. She loves to goad her father. She says I could use a little competition. I'd started my own firm a number of years back, and we'd won a couple of fairly high-profile class-action suits. Lily is as blond as her sister is dark and a true beauty, a fact that she seems to be entirely oblivious to—even if, to my chagrin, the boys on campus are not. Now, Hannah was bringing the baby home for his first Christmas.

Kate has been sent into a tailspin, readying the house for her girls and her new grandson.

"Move that over there, Robert," she says, only to change her mind a few seconds later, "No, move it back. It takes up too much room over there." I can scarcely keep up with her as she drags me along, baking and cooking in the kitchen, running to the attic for decorations, and shopping for Christmas presents for the baby.

"Our first Christmas with our grandchild," she squeals into my ear.

It seems what I'd always heard is true: You become a crazy person when you turn into a grandparent. Our refrigerator was already covered with pictures of Evan, smiling up at the camera from the tub, from the floor, from the crib, and from the car seat. Basically, it's the same picture—just a different location each time.

When the car pulled up in the driveway this after-noon, Kate shoved me out of the way and rushed out the door, her arms waving high above her head. "Merry Christmas!" she shouted, making a beeline for the car. After a quick round of hugging and kissing Hannah and Steven, Kate gingerly scooped up the baby and lifted him high into the air.

"There he is!" she exclaimed. "There's Grandma's boy!" Hannah ran to me and planted a big kiss on my cheek before grabbing the baby's bag off the backseat. Together, she and Kate made their way into the house, oohing and ahhing over the baby, closing the door firmly behind them. Steven and I just looked at each other and laughed.

"Well, Merry Christmas to you too!" I yelled toward the door. Glancing at my watch, I said, "Steven, since we'll never be missed in there," motioning toward the house, "how about riding with me to pick up Lily at the airport?"

When we returned, the house was aglow with the Christmas lights and decorations I had put up the weekend following Thanksgiving. Kate oversaw the whole production, yelling up to me on the ladder "Those lights are sagging too much" or "Robert, move the wreath over toward the center of the window a hair." By the end of the day, the house was something Mother would have been proud of, complete with her yard sale Nativity lighting the front lawn. Lily burst through the front door, sweeping her nephew into her arms, gently tapping his small nose, exclaiming, "Look at you! Look at you!"

I pulled out the Dunhill Billiard and packed the cylinder bowl with tobacco that smelled like a forest of pine trees. I puffed on the plastic bit till the tobacco caught, flicking my right hand to put out the match. "Dad!" Lily whined. "Do you have to light that thing?" But Kate didn't say a word. She never knew why I sporadically smoked the pipe, but she never asked either. All she knew was it had something to do with bringing me back to her. And that's all she needed to know.

Evan giggled as Kate raised him high in the air, then brought him down toward her, sticking her nose in his round belly.

"Who's Grandma's angel?" she asked in a voice that, I imagine, alerted every dog in the neighborhood. "Who's Grandma's angel?" The baby laughed and gurgled, his tiny arms and legs wiggling in the air. Lily offered her finger for Evan to grab and proceeded to bounce his hand around like that of a tiny orchestra conductor, while Kate lifted him repeatedly up and down, up and down.

I sat back, puffing on the pipe, and smiled at what we'd become, a family, and wondered again what had happened to the small boy with the Christmas shoes who'd changed my life forever.

EPILOGUE

Christmas, 2000

The wind whipped at my face as I knelt down and carefully wiped the clumps of frozen leaves from the base of the tombstone. "Ellen Katherine Layton," it read. "August 15, 1917–December 26, 1985. Beloved Mother." I cleared the area in front of the stone as well and made the short trek back to the base of the hill. I opened the trunk of my car to retrieve some of my mother's favorite Christmas decorations: poinsettias, holly, and an evergreen wreath. Slipping the wreath up my arm and over my shoulder, I caught a glimpse of someone else in the cemetery. It occurred to me that it was an odd day to visit a cemetery. As a matter of fact, in all my years of visiting my mother's grave, I couldn't remember ever seeing anyone else here on Christmas Day. I shrugged, hoping the poor soul was warmer than I was, and closed the trunk.

Trudging back to the grave, the wind shrieked in my bare ears. I put my head down to avoid the icy lashing, shrinking my neck into the warmth of the coat collar. As I passed, I could see that the other man was holding a brown paper sack. I briefly caught the nice-looking young man's eyes. He was slender and tall, wearing a thick, navy down parka and a wool hat with a university logo on it.

"Morning," I said, waving my arm full of decorations toward the man.

"Good morning," the young man waved. "Merry Christmas!"

"Merry Christmas to you," I cheerily replied.

"You're the first person I've seen here on Christmas Day in years!" the young man yelled above the winds.

"I was just thinking the same thing!" I shouted.

The wind died down a bit, and the sun beamed, lighting the ice-covered boughs and tombstones until the whole cemetery shone.

"Did you go to the university?" I asked, gesturing toward his hat.

"Yes, still do," he responded with a smile.

"Class of seventy!" I replied, patting my chest. "We were still using inkwells back then, of course. What are you studying?"

"Oncology," he said somewhat shyly. "If I can stick it out, that is."

"Terrific. Pretty tough program, though. These roads are something, aren't they? I couldn't get up the hill here at all," I exclaimed.

"Yes, sir. I was just down Route Ten from the hospital. They've sanded, but it's not doing much. Maybe this sun will help."

"They've got you on call already?" I chuckled. The wind began to pick up again. I wrapped my coat tighter.

"Oh no, not yet," he laughed. The young man had warm, blue eyes; his cheeks were red from the cold. "I just do a little volunteer work there when I'm home from school."

"That's great. The hospital's no place to be on Christmas. I'm sure the patients appreciate you, though. Well, nice speaking to you. You have a Merry Christmas," I said, quickening my pace back to my mother's grave.

"Thank you, you too, Merry Christmas," he said.

I draped the holly over the top of the tombstone. I positioned the evergreen wreath to the left of the lettering and placed a poinsettia directly in front of it, with a matching poinsettia positioned to the right. Scratching at the stone, I dug out the frost that was wedged into the lettering. "There," I said, whisking any remnants away as I leaned back to admire my work. "She'd like that," I assured myself.

I know that most people decorated grave sites on Memorial Day, but my mother loved Christmas, not Memorial Day, so regardless of whether it was thirty-five degrees or thirty-five below zero, I made my way to the cemetery each year and decorated her stone, always placing an extra poinsettia on my father's stone beside her.

"It's awfully cold this Christmas, Mom," I said, banging my hands together. "I know someone who must have been extremely grateful for not having to decorate your house this year," I laughed, picturing the retired Dalton teetering on one of Mother's rickety ladders while she barked out the precise placement of each decoration.

"Hannah brought Evan home, and I'm not too proud to say he takes after his granddad in many ways: good-looking, suave . . . has a certain charm with the ladies. Oh, and did I mention modest? You'll meet him one day and see the similarities for yourself." I paused, looking again at the year of death.

"I still miss you, Mom," I shivered. "I miss you every day."

I stood to go and noticed that the other man had already left. Probably couldn't take the cold, I thought. Bracing myself against the wind, I started back down the hill when something caught my eye at the grave where the man had been standing. Approaching the car, I strained to see what had been placed on the tombstone. As I moved closer, my heart began to pound. I quickened my pace and saw that at the base of the stone lay a brand-new pair of glittery, beaded shoes. I quickly read the name on the marker and the date of death: "Margaret Elizabeth Andrews. March 17, 1951–December 25, 1985. Beloved Wife-Mother-Daughter."

I spun around in the direction of where the young man's car had been parked, but the cemetery was empty. His car was gone. So I placed one of Mother's poinsettias alongside the shoes on the tombstone, and drove home.

Smiling.

AFTERWORD
Today

If we're open to it, God can use even the smallest thing to change our lives . . . to change us. It might be a laughing child, car brakes that need fixing, a sale on pot roast, a cloudless sky, a trip to the woods to cut down a Christmas tree, a schoolteacher, a Dunhill Billiard pipe . . . or even a pair of shoes.

Some people will never believe. They may feel that such things are too trivial, too simple, or too insignificant to forever change a life. But I believe.

And I always will.

"THE CHRISTMAS SHOES"

by Eddie Carswell and Leonard Ahlstrom

It was almost Christmas time
And there I stood in another line
Trying to buy that last gift or two
Not really in the Christmas mood
Standing right in front of me
Was a little boy waiting anxiously
Pacing round like little boys do
And in his hands, he held a pair of shoes

And his clothes were worn and old
He was dirty from head to toe
And when it came his time to pay
I couldn't believe what I heard him say

CHORUS

Sir, I want to buy these shoes
For my momma, please
It's Christmas Eve and these shoes are just her size
Could you hurry, sir
Daddy says there's not much time
You see she's been sick for quite a while
And I know these shoes will make her smile
And I want her to look beautiful
If momma meets Jesus tonight

They counted pennies for what seemed like years
Then the cashier said, son, there's not enough here
He searched his pockets frantically
And then he turned and he looked at me
He said, momma made Christmas good at our house
Though, most years, she just did without
Tell me, sir, what am I going to do
Somehow I've got to buy her these Christmas shoes

So I laid the money down
I just had to help him out
And I'll never forget the look on his face
When he said momma's gonna look so great

REPEAT CHORUS

I knew I caught a glimpse of heaven's love
As he thanked me and ran out
I knew that God had sent that little boy
To remind me what Christmas is all about

REPEAT CHORUS

Center Point Publishing
600 Brooks Road ● PO Box 1
Thorndike ME 04986-0001 USA

(207) 568-3717

US & Canada:
1 800 929-9108